Frank Benson turned .... or-
ward, head ducked, to open the livery door wide
enough for Edge to lead his horse outside.

A man shouted, "Now, damnit!"

Hoofbeats hit the street, just discernible through the
storm sounds and the splashing of puddled rainwater
kicked up by the pumping legs of the galloping
horses.

Sheet lightning flashed and thunder cracked. Murk
that was close to night dark was for a split second
changed into a brightness the sun could never match,
and showed Lester, Rico, and Elmer in stark clarity,
crouched low in their saddles as they raced their
mounts in a single file along the center of the street.
West to east. Each with his right arm held across the
front of his chest, hand fisted around the butt of a revolver.

"Benson!" Edge shouted, letting go of the bridle of
his horse to turn and reach for the scabbarded Winchester.

Benson started to bring up his head, but there was
no time for any other voluntary move. For the lightning flash was gone and he could see nothing but
lancing drops of rain for the moment before muzzle
flashes—mere short-lived streaks through the sodden
gloom—signaled the approach of bullets toward him.

"It ain't—"

Benson was hit and cried out more in surprise than
pain. The gelding took a bullet and gave a body-
shuddering snort as the half-breed slid the rifle from
the scabbard.

Edge steeled himself for what was to come. They had
just killed an innocent man because he stood in the
way . . . and Edge knew that *he* was their real target
. . .

THE EDGE SERIES:

Best-Selling Series!

#41 The Most Violent
Westerns in Print

EDGE

THE KILLING CLAIM

BY

George G. Gilman

PINNACLE BOOKS NEW YORK

EDGE #41: THE KILLING CLAIM

Copyright © 1982 by George G. Gilman

A Pinnacle Book, first published in Great Britain by New English Library Limited in 1982.

First printing, December 1982

ISBN: 0-523-41924-4

Cover illustration by Bruce Menney

Printed in the United States of America

PINNACLE BOOKS, INC.
1430 Broadway
New York, New York 10018

For:
S. an inspiration of a different color.

THE KILLING CLAIM

Chapter One

The man called Edge continued to sit astride the bay gelding while the horse drank from the cool, crystal-clear water of Mirror Lake. Rolled a cigarette with the makings taken from a pocket of his shirt and lit it with a match struck on the butt of the Frontier Colt that jutted from the holster tied down to his right thigh. Through the smoke that curled up from the cigarette angled from a corner of his mouth, he peered dispassionately across the mile-wide lake to the community on the north shore. Then, turning his narrow-eyed gaze to the left and to the right, he surveyed the shoreline on this side of the lake, in search of the best route around the expanse of water sparkling in the sun of noon to the town on the far side.

To both the west and the east the lake curved out of sight beyond timber-clad hills, the kind of fir-covered rises he had ridden around or over for more than a week. And much the same as those which half circled the town of Lakeview that was so close as the crow flies, but untold hours or maybe even days away on a swing to the west or east. Depending upon what kind of terrain was concealed by the timber that crowded the lake-shore.

He took a dime from a pocket of his pants, flipped it, and caught it, pressed it with the palm of his right hand against the back of his left.

"Heads west," he muttered.

The gelding finished drinking and the man in the saddle raised his right hand to see that the dime had come down to show tails. The horse vented a snort and Edge took the cigarette from his mouth and drew back his lips to show his teeth in a grin that did not inject any warmth into the slits of his eyes.

"If that was a horselaugh, feller," he growled softly, "maybe you've forgotten the joke's on you. And there's no way to make light of that."

He replaced the cigarette between his lips and tugged gently on the reins to turn the horse towards the east. A two-hundred-pound burden to the gelding that had carried him a lot of miles on this trip from Stormville in the new state of Colorado to within sight of Lakeview, Territory of Montana. By way of Denver and then Cheyenne. On stage or freight trails for some of the way. But mostly cutting across the rugged country of the Continental Divide's eastern flank when the trails swung too wide of the direction he had in mind to go.

Two hundred pounds of weight stacked six feet three inches high in a manner that gave Edge a lean build that matched the cut of his features. Features that offered more than a subtle suggestion that their form was the result of the mingling of two racial bloodlines—the Hispanic of his Mexican father and the Aryan of his Swedish mother. Into the flesh that was stained as much by heritage as exposure to the elements was set a pair of eyes that were ice blue. And framing the face with its high cheekbones, hawklike nose, thin-lipped mouth, and firm jaw was a growth of thick, jet black hair that hung down to brush his shoulders.

It was a face that had been inscribed with many deep lines during the almost forty years of the man's life, some put there by the aging process but as many by the harsh experiences of living the kind of life his ruling fates had decreed for him.

In total, it was a face that could be regarded as either handsome or ugly, depending upon how one viewed the coldly penetrating gaze of the always narrowed eyes, and the more than vague hint of cruelty suggested by the thin lips when in repose. This truthful indication of one of the man's character traits emphasized by the way he wore a just discernible Mexican-style moustache, which this late in the day was almost impossible to see against the morning's growth of dark bristles on his lower face.

He was dressed for the kind of country through which he rode and for the chill of the fall air up here in the Rockies just to the south of the international border with Canada. Wore a black Stetson, a gray shirt, blue denim pants with the cuffs outside the spurless black riding boots, and a knee-length sheepskin coat that was not fastened—and thus did not impede access to the holstered Colt.

Nor to the open straight razor that he carried in a sheath held at the nape of his neck by a beaded thong encircling his throat.

While, should danger threaten from longer range, his right hand resting on the saddlehorn to hold the reins was only inches away from the stock of a Winchester rifle that jutted from the forward-hung scabbard.

Moving along a twenty-foot-wide strip of soft, dry sand that caved into the indentations each time the gelding raised a hoof for a new stride, the man called Edge seemed only superficially interested in the surroundings as occasionally he shifted his attention from the way ahead to glance in other directions. For he revealed no sign by his apparently relaxed manner that he was prepared at a split second's notice to respond to a threat from any quarter. He relied as much on his well-honed sixth sense as on the evidence of his eyes and ears to warn him of imminent danger.

Was prepared by countless brushes with death to be ready to face and defeat any new menace that might be waiting to attack him on this sun-bright, fall-cold day.

He heard the sound while he was still a quarter-mile short of where the sandy lakeshore disappeared beyond the steep shoulder of a hill. And shifted his eyes lazily along the narrowest of slits to look in the direction from which the howl had come. Which was close to the top of the rise, in the thick of the Douglas fir trees that cloaked the slope. This as he reined the gelding to a halt and removed the nearly smoked cigarette from his lips to arc it out into the lake.

The horse stood quietly, but Edge was aware of the rigidity of the animal's stance, and he sought to calm him by running a hand down the stretched neck as another howl reverberated from the timber. It continued for much longer than before, the variable pitch emphasizing that it was a distress call.

"You figure a wolf, feller?" Edge said to his mount, speaking softly and using the tone of his voice to augment the calming effect of his stroking hand. But then the howl was curtailed and was followed by several sharp barks. And Edge added, "Or a hound, maybe?"

The gelding snorted and tossed his head, obviously eager to start moving again and get out of earshot of a fellow creature in distress.

The half-breed, still speaking to ease the anxiety of the horse, said: "You're right, feller. Whatever his problem is, it ain't ours."

He gently heeled the horse into movement, but needed to ride with a tight rein to keep him from choosing a gallop.

The dog continued to howl and bark by turns; the sounds made the more insistent in the ears of Edge because they came constantly from the same spot on the timbered slope. Edge grimaced and concentrated solely on the way ahead, struggling to bar from his mind the nagging thought that the dog was pleading for help because it was injured and in pain.

Then he was carried around the shoulder of the hill and the gelding came to a halt of his own accord. A wall of rock jutted out of the trees, across the strip of sand, and reached some thirty feet into the lake in the form of a twenty-foot high, timber-topped promontory. Around the base of which the water rippled soothingly, in dramatic contrast to the sounds being vented by the distressed dog.

Edge surveyed the barrier with a cold-eyed gaze but with the trace of a smile turning up the corners of his lips as he stroked the neck of his horse and drawled, "Seems like the spin of the coin had us barking up the wrong tree, feller."

He tugged on the reins to command a slow wheel and, as he rode back around the shoulder of the hill, he glanced across at the community which hugged a half-mile length of shoreline on the north side of the lake. The howling of the dog had stirred up no noticeable activity on the waterfront street with its two piers to which a half dozen small boats were moored. But then neither had his appearance on the shore at this side of the lake caused any disturbance in the town, short of a barely perceptible interruption in the mundane daily activity along the lakeside street when he was first spotted riding out of the timber.

He turned his back on Lakeview to return to the cold shade of the trees at the start of the climb toward the dog, which had begun to whimper and whine rather than howl and bark. The difference in temperature between sunlight ane shade was marked, so he buttoned his coat and turned up its collar after first transferring the Colt from the holster to a pocket.

For most of the time he was able to ride in an almost direct line from the lake toward the dog, veering only slightly from one side to the other to go between the towering trunks of the Douglas firs. On just three occasions needed to go off at an acute tangent across the steeply rising ground to get past an impenetrable clump of brush and two lichen-covered granite crags.

He remained in the saddle, even though the going would have been easier had he dismounted. The extra concentration this demanded from the gelding helped to keep his equine mind off the less frequent but still disturbing cries of the dog. Which grew louder by degrees as the distance to the troubled animal narrowed.

Then, fifteen cold minutes after the climb had started, the dog heard the sounds of the horse and rider approaching. Curtailed a whine and, after a few stretched seconds of silence, vented a low-pitched growl. That grew into a snarl.

Edge stopped the horse and, pushing his right hand into his coat pocket, fisted it around the butt of the Colt. He tilted his head back to look up at the rim of a thirty-foot-high granite escarpment, above which he could see only sky. From beyond came the sound of the dog's fear-charged aggression.

The sheer face of the cliff was the most severe obstacle he had yet come up against. But at least there was no choice to be made about direction. To the north was a complete barrier, since it was the promontory that jutted out into the lake. So he turned the nervous gelding toward the south, maintaining for as long as he was able an impassive watch on the cliff top, and not relaxing his grip on the Colt until the dog became silent and timber once again concealed the escarpment.

Gradually, as the ground Edge rode over rose, the two levels merged and he was able to steer the horse around a clump of evergreen brush and head back north again. To close with the now silent dog. Riding with his hand on the gun in his pocket once more, his narrowed eyes peered ahead, seeking a break in the trees that would offer him first sight of the animal which continued to remain ominously quiet.

Rounding a small outcrop of rock, Edge saw the dog. Abandoned the Colt and reached to slide the Winchester from the scabbard as the gelding wheeled and reared in terror.

It was the largest German shepherd the half-breed had ever seen. At one instant down in a quivering crouch, silent and staring. The next galvanized into a run that was planned to power a leap at both man and horse, unwelcome strangers in the clearing on the top of the escarpment. A clearing perhaps a hundred feet long by forty wide. Half circled by the trunks of the firs to the north and the east. Concealed from the west by the tops of the trees growing on a slope at the base of the cliff. With just a very narrow access from the south between the outcrop and the rim of the sheer drop. At its center a small, crude log cabin that had doubtless been built with the lumber of the trees felled to form the clearing.

All this glimpsed between two blinks of the slitted, glittering blue eyes. The backdrop to the dog's vicious attack checked to insure that the animal was the only danger. Between the last and the next brief coming together of eyelids, the situation seen in its entirety. And the priorities for survival were altered.

The big dog with the bared fangs and the iridescent eyes sprang up from the ground, body and legs at full stretch and on course for the exposed neck of the rearing horse.

The gelding, his snort of fear masking the snarl of the attacking dog, beat at the air with his forelegs and struggled to turn on the strained rear ones.

Edge thrust the rifle back into the scabbard before it was halfway out and took hold of the reins in both hands. Using his heels and elbows in concert with the reins, he brought the horse down four footed again, wrenching his head and body around in the opposite direction from the way he wanted to turn—which would have plunged himself and his rider over the rim of the escarpment. The gelding responded to the commands of the man astride him and came down hard and heavy on his forelegs.

The German shepherd leaped, but the powerful forward momentum was abruptly halted in midair as the rope that tethered him to the hook on the cabin wall pulled taut. The dog slammed to the ground, yelping with pain and frustration, less than six feet from the now rearing forehooves of the panicked gelding.

Snickering and moving his head up and down in a pumping action, the horse backed and sidled away from the dog. In danger now of losing his footing with his shaking hindlegs.

Edge rasped a curse and kicked free of one stir-

rup. To swing across and out of the saddle. This
as he arced a hand wide, to take the reins forward
to the animal's head during a dipping mo-
tion. And, as soon as he was on the ground, he
dropped into a crouch and braced himself. The
reins gripped in both hands now—to haul the
gelding back from the top of the cliff.

The dog sprang up snarling and, the saliva of
boundless rage flying from his jaws, commanded
the total attention of the larger animal. Which,
with pricked ears, flared nostrils, wide lips, and
bulged eyes, moved inexorably toward the sheer
drop.

The man's booted feet slithered across the lush
turf at the base of the outcrop.

The gelding's hooves scraped on the bare rock
at the very top of the cliff.

The German shepherd, at full stretch as he
strained at the tether, dug the claws of all four
paws into the hard-packed dirt of the clearing.

Curses, snarls, and snorts were loud in the surrounding silence.

The half-breed experienced the cold sweat of
fear beading his every pore as he faced his di-
lemma: whether to take a hand off the reins to
draw the Colt and put a bullet through the head of
the rage-maddened dog, or to keep wrenching
with both hands in the hope that brute strength
would eventually have an effect.

The sight of the dog twitching into death amid a
spray of blood could perhaps expand the gelding's panic. But the relentless way in which the
terrified horse was moving toward the top of the
drop seemed to make it certain that Edge had no

chance of holding him. So there was nothing to lose in trying to save the horse by blasting the dog.

A fresh sound made itself heard through the cursing, the snarling, and the snorting. A piercingly shrill whistle that had an instant effect on the dog, which sat down on his haunches and began to whine pathetically as he licked the saliva off his jaws.

The half-breed curtailed his soft venting of obscenities as he retightened his grip on the reins and leaned back harder with his heels digging deep into the turf.

The horse became motionless, although still ignoring the man to stare down at the dog—fear giving way to confusion.

A second short whistle, less shrill, brought the dog to his feet. He strolled back to the front of the cabin, where, below an open window to the right of the closed door, he whimpered once before he turned around three times and lay down, body curled and legs tucked under him. Jaws free of saliva now, eyes an appealing brown, and ears back along his head. Utterly docile.

The gelding vented a low snort and a quiver went through him.

Edge straightened and stroked the neck of the horse as he tugged gently on the reins to ease the animal back from the brink of the drop. But took care not to put himself or the calming animal within range of the tethered dog. While all the time he kept close watch on the partially opened sash window from which the two command whistles had been emitted.

Then a man who sounded old and weak called
from the shade-darkened interior of the cabin:
"Don't reckon this is my lucky day, is it? That ain't
you, Ralph? Or Lee? Or the both of you?"

The dog was panting after his exertions, tongue
lolling out at the side. At the sound of the man's
voice he pricked his ears, raised his head, and
cocked it, to look with longing expectancy up at
the window.

"That's right, feller!" Edge called back. "It
ain't Ralph or Lee!"

"Then best you don't come no closer to the
place, stranger! Or I'll set the hound on you!"

He still sounded old and sickly weak, but there
was determination in his voice. His dog dis-
cerned the change of tone—snapped his head
down and around to watch the intruders. Prepared to attack again.

"No sweat!" Edge answered and led the calm
but wary horse along the fringe of the clearing
beyond the rock outcrop. Needing to move into
the danger area of the dog's range for several
yards. So kept one hand in his pocket, the palm
greasy with sweat, on the butt of the uncocked revolver.

"What's that supposed to mean?"

"For you not to sweat, I guess, feller! Figure I'm
doing enough for the both of us!"

"Hey, you've moved. Ain't no use you tryin' to
get in the back of the place, stranger! Hound
can't get at you back there, but there ain't no door
or windows!"

The cabin was built at an angle across the center of the clearing, facing the rock outcrop at the southwest corner along which Edge was leading the horse, watched every inch of the way by the dog poised to lunge forward again.

Then the rock curved away and there was yielding brush to offer an escape out of range of the canine threat. But it offered scant defense against a volley of gunfire should the old man decide he needed to take his suspicion of the intruder that seriously.

Edge turned to cut the corner of the clearing, moving parallel with the windowless side of the cabin.

"Listen, mister! I ain't got nothin' here at the place that's worth more than a few cents! And I didn't mean that about settin' the hound on you! I called him off the first time, didn't I? And I didn't set him on you! I was asleep, see! First I knowed there was someone outside the place was when the ruckus woke me! You got a gun, I bet?"

He sounded close to tears. Perhaps too close. Overplaying the part of a frightened old-timer at the mercy of a stranger who means him no good. So Edge stayed fully alert to the possibility that the man in the cabin had a gun and was awaiting the right opportunity to use it. He peered unblinkingly at the side and then the rear wall of the cabin, in search of a hole or a crack through which the barrel of a revolver or a rifle could be jutted. While all the time he moved toward a gap in the trees at the far corner of the clearing, which could well be the start of a pathway around the lake to the town.

"And I reckon that if I did set the hound on you again, mister—well, I reckon you'd use that gun to kill him! Wouldn't you, I bet?"

There was a weed-choked vegetable patch on the far side of the clearing with the remains of just a few neglected rows of crops struggling to survive. Edge led his horse around the side of this and reached the twenty-foot-wide gap in the trees. Allowed a brief smile of satisfaction to draw his lips fractionally apart when he saw that it was the start of a little-used trail. Which curved down from the high ground to give access to the lakeshore on the far side of the promontory.

He swung up astride the no longer nervous gelding and made to heel his mount away from the clearing and on to the trail.

The old man in the cabin called, "Help me, stranger!"

Edge stayed the move to leave and looked back over his shoulder at the windowless rear and side of his crude home. Convinced by the degree of pleading in the voice that the old man inside was not acting. Then, after stretched seconds of frowning thought, he swung down from the saddle. Hitched the horse to a clump of brush and moved with long, silent strides toward the cabin. Drew the Colt out of his pocket but did not cock it when he reached the front corner, just fifteen feet away from where the dog lay.

The animal had heard his approach and was tensed to move against him, eyes afire with latent viciousness, ears pricked, and fangs bared. He growled and brought the still frowning man to within a part of a second of killing him. But the sound of the old man's voice, low and bitter, caused the big German shepherd to become wearily docile again. He even yawned as he lowered his head to the ground between his front paws, totally ignoring the man with the aimed gun.

"Easy there, old buddy. That stone-hearted sonofabitch don't wanna lend us a hand, that's his loss. We'll make out, same as we always have. And I promise you this, boy, before I cash in my chips, I'll cut you loose. We don't need nobody else when we got each—shit, mister, what's the idea of creepin' up on a man like that?"

"Didn't mean to, feller," Edge answered as he peered through the other, unopened window in the facade of the cabin. But the glass was too dirty and he could see nothing clearly. "Can't help it if I'm the quiet type."

"Suits me fine if you've a mind to come in and sit a spell, stranger," the old man replied with a note of eagerness now. "Just need you to listen to what I gotta say. And after I'm through sayin' it, you only gotta answer me yes or no."

"Take long?"

"Few minutes to tell. Rest of your life to reap the benefits, mister. What d'you say?"

"Not a thing for a few minutes," Edge answered and moved away from the dirt-smeared window to the door.

As he reached forward with his free hand to lift the latch, the dog raised his head, turned it, and vented another warning growl through his bared fangs.

The man beyond the door soothed: "Easy, old buddy, Friend."

The dog allowed his tongue to loll out and began to thump the ground with his tail. And immediately looked as trustingly innocent and harmless as a puppy.

"That's fine, feller. I like most animals better than I like most people," the half-breed said to the dog.

He pushed the Colt back into his coat pocket and hinged open the door with his other hand. Came close to gagging on the stench that assaulted his nostrils from inside the cabin.

"Except when they try to put the bite on me," he added.

Chapter Two

"Thought you said you was the quiet type, mister?" the old man complained with acid sarcasm as Edge shifted this gaze from the placid dog to the interior of the evil-smelling cabin, now much better lit with the sunlight that angled down through the open doorway.

"Fine, feller. From now until you're through, it'll be like the cat's got my tongue."

The German shepherd abruptly sprang to his feet, lips curled back from his saliva, gleaming fangs, every hair bristling as he vented the most menacing snarl yet. Then, as when Edge had first rode into sight around the outcrop of rock at the top of the cliff, the animal launched into the attack.

But the half-breed had reacted the moment the dog signaled the start of this new explosion of viciousness. Stepped across the threshold and slammed the door before the dog was four footed. And was leaning his back against the inside of the door when the animal slammed a shoulder into the outside. Remained in this position, grimacing

with ice-cold anger, while the dog bounced off
the door with a yelp of pain and raced away from
the cabin. Yelped louder when he was again
jerked to an abrupt halt by the tether.

"Easy, old buddy!" the old man cried, the effort required to shout the command causing a fit
of coughing to rack his body.

When it was ended, the dog could be heard
padding back to his accustomed place below the
partly opened window, panting and whining.

"What happened?" Edge asked, a modicum of
the cold anger that glittered in the slits of his
hooded eyes sounding in his voice.

"Weren't my fault," the old man answered
quickly and defensively. "Nor his. Nor yours neither, I guess. You couldn't know that he always
acts that way to anyone who mentions . . ." He
lowered his voice to a rasping whisper to add,
"Cats."

"Anything else I should know to keep me from
having to shoot your dog?"

"No, mister. Long as you don't mention them
other animals again and give me no reason to set
him on you, he'll be the same with you as he is
with me."

Edge nodded and reached inside his coat to
take the makings from a shirt pocket as he raked
his eyes over the single, twenty-by-ten-foot room
that was all the cabin contained.

It was as spartanly furnished as it was crudely
built. Had a hard-packed dirt floor and walls and
peaked ceiling of untreated logs with chunks of
time-loosened bark hanging from many of them.
Against the rear wall, directly opposite the door

where Edge continued to stand, was a potbellied stove without a fire in it. In the center of the half room to the left was an arrangement of wooden crates that served as a table with a backless bench along one side. Close to, but not under, the partly opened window in the other half of the room was a narrow bed in which the old man half sat and half lay, uncomfortably propped up against the iron frame of the bedhead, naked above the waist and with a blanket draped over his belly and legs.

The man looked very sick as well as old, with a grotesquely thin torso and arms in which every bone seemed to be sharply contoured by almost translucent skin. There was a skeletal quality about his totally hairless head too. But instead of being dough gray in color and smooth in texture, the skin that draped his dome and the bone structure of his face was stained a dark brown by countless hours of exposure to the elements and was heavily crinkled by the hard-to-estimate years of his living.

He did not move, even to blink his tiny eyes nor to moisten his cracked and arid lips, while Edge rolled a cigarette and lit it with a match struck on the frame of the door. And it would have been easy to assume that he had suddenly died. Which, Edge reflected as he drew deeply against the cigarette, would be the best thing that could happen for both of them. The ancient because he could surely have nothing good left to live for, and his visitor, who could then get out of the cabin, with its nauseatingly fetid atmosphere that threatened to expel from deep within the half-breed something more solid than the tobacco smoke that now trickled from a corner of his compressed lips.

"Name's Barny Galton and I wanna thank you for droppin' by, mister."

Edge nodded shortly as he sucked in and exhaled more smoke. Seeking to calm his churning stomach and hopeful the smoke would go some way toward masking the evil stench that emanated from the bed.

"You got a name?"

"Edge, feller."

"You got the look of a Mexican about you."

"From my pa, feller. You want to get said what needs to be said? So I can get on over to Lakeview."

"Somethin' special for you over in that place, Mr. Edge?"

"Hopeful of stores where I can get some supplies. You want to cover yourself better against the cold? So I can open the door."

Galton's crinkled face had been totally expressionless until now, the loose skin at his throat more animated than his lips when he spoke. But after the question was asked, he arranged his features into the form of a puzzled frown. Which lasted for perhaps two seconds before a look of disgust displaced it.

"Guess I smell real bad by now, Mr. Edge?"

"Can't recall the time I ever came across any man who smelled worse, feller. That wasn't dead."

Now the old man expressed self-pity as he defended "It ain't just that I made a mess in the bed.

And I couldn't help doin' that, mister. On account of the accident."

And now he grimaced with the effort needed to move one of his wasted arms, the skin-and-bone hand rising into a claw. But he was too weak even to clutch at the blanket he wanted to drag off his legs.

"I've smelled gangrene almost as many times as I've smelled shit, feller. And seen enough poisoned wounds to last me a lifetime. There a doctor in Lakeview?"

The cracked lips were drawn back from gums in which just six or so teeth were still rooted. And Barny Galton's naked chest and belly tremored with draining laughter.

Edge waited with patience for the inevitable end result. And then continued to keep his back to the door while he smoked the cigarette as the emaciated old man was painfully racked by a fit of hacking coughing. Then said evenly, "Like what's left of your life, feller, the few minutes you mentioned are running out fast."

Galton tried to breathe deeply in the hope of speeding his recovery from the exhausting bout of coughing. But this was itself another drain on his diminished resources, and his anguish brought tears from his eyes. And he squeezed them tightly shut and began to talk very fast.

"If I can hang on until midnight, I'll be eighty-nine, mister. Like to do that, but it ain't so important to me. Be good to die here at the place where I been for forty-nine years, come tomorrow. Like, too, for somebody to take care of the dog after my

time's up. You can open up the door if you like,
mister. I don't feel the cold no more. Just like I
ain't smelled myself for a long time now. You figure I'll get them kinda things back before I cash
in? Or maybe I'll go blind and deaf as well before
the end?"

"I figure you can't tell, feller," Edge answered.
"Does different things to different people."

He kept the door closed and, after he dropped
the butt of the cigarette to the dirt floor, made the
act of crushing it out the first step toward the
stove.

"But you ain't got the time for that kinda talk,
Mr. Edge," the dying man went on, eyes still
closed and Adam's apple moving more than his
lips to voice the words. "You come into the place
to hear how me cashin' in can make you rich."

Edge dropped to his haunches before the stove
and grunted with satisfaction when he saw a fire
had been laid inside. He struck the match on the
side of the stove and lit the kindling. It caught immediately, tinder dry from having been in the
stove for several days.

"I told you I don't feel the cold no more!" Galton said in a tone that was almost vehement as he
stared with eyes that were briefly glittering at the
man who came erect beside the stove.

"People who take time to die usually feel the
cold real bad, feller."

"So what the hell if I freeze the other leg off?"
the old man demanded. He could not maintain his
anger, and after a long pause for several breaths
he spoke in the familiar rasping tone. "I ain't

askin' not a thing of you except that you listen, Mr. Edge."

The half-breed nodded slowly several times as he peered at the blanket-draped contours of Galton's lower body and saw that the stained and crusted fabric covered just the thigh and knee of the man's left leg.

"How long ago, Mr. Galton?"

The old man shifted his head slightly to look at the filthy window just above and a little to the side of his left shoulder, where six lines had been inscribed in the dirt. "Counted six sunrises since I got to this bed, Mr. Edge. Ain't so certain how long I was in the mine after the cave-in. Black as pitch down there and I kept comin' and goin'. Unconscious like, for a lot of the time."

Edge nodded again. "Guess the idea of me bringing a doctor from town was pretty funny, feller."

"Funniest thing since I give the dog my leg to eat. When I was still strong enough to take off the boot and push it out through the window here. Before the meat got too rotten."

There had been a number of times during the more violent periods of his life when the man called Edge had experienced the eerie sensation of being in the grip of a waking dream—or nightmare. Starkly aware of what was happening to him and yet not quite able to believe that it was credible. But never had he felt more strongly than now that he was the only subject of substance in a situation of otherwise absolute unreality.

"See, not bein' able to get myself any food, that
didn't bother me none," Barny Galton went on in
a tone that would have been matter-of-fact had it
not been forced to sound weak and rasping. "Last
thing I been feelin' is hungry, I can tell you.
Thirsty some, at first. Not even that for a long
time. But the dog. I had to feed my old buddy. It
was real lucky it rained a time or two so that his
drinkin' bowl got refilled."

The dying old man was entering a state of calm
delirium that had an almost hypnotic effect on
Edge. He felt a powerful urge to get out of the
cabin but was rooted to the spot, while in a part of
his mind he conjured up vivid images of what had
happened to the man.

Saw a mind picture of him falling under a del-
uge of crumbling rock. Then of him crawling
through the wooded country to this cabin in the
clearing. Leaving a bloody trail from the terrible
wound where half a leg had been torn loose.
Clutching the dismembered part of the leg for no
logical reason because his agony-assaulted mind
could not possibly process rational thoughts.
Reaching the cabin to be greeted by the big German shepherd. Coming inside and now feeling
something in addition to awesome pain. Shivering in a cold sweat, so closing the door. Dragging
himself over to and up on to the bed. Still hug-
ging the detached part of his leg.

Later emptying his bowels and his bladder,
helplessly trapped in the bed. Then being made
to face up to the inevitable realization when the
stink of his own waste became combined with a

more awful stench—given off by his own flesh decomposing before he was dead.

The high peak of agony was perhaps past by then. And perhaps he could feel no pain at all. Which would have made the howling of his starving dog that much harder to bear.

And then came the most vivid and yet unbelievable image of all—of Barny Galton turning on the bed, raising the window, pushing the lower half of his leg through, and almost closing the window again as the ravenous animal gorged on the human meat.

Was it then that the fever hit the old man and caused him to tear the clothing off his emaciated body? Or had that happened while he sweated through the deadly attack of gangrene?

Or maybe the image Edge had received of the pus beginning to infect the wound had been out of chronological order. . .

But what did it matter?

What difference did it make that he had experienced similar sensations of being present and yet detached from events in the past?

What was important was that he knew for certain he was awake. Standing in a log cabin in northern Montana. Having just lit a fire in a stove so that a man who would soon die would have no reason to feel any brand of cold unless it be from the stirring of the air by the wings of the Angel of Death.

"But none of that matters, mister," Barny Galton was saying, to cut in on the series of images Edge struggled to blot out. "Thing is that if I was a

religious man, you'd be the answer to the prayers
I would've been offerin' up. And this is what you
gotta do."

The half-breed felt compelled to look toward
the dying man and then sensed his gaze was held
in a trap by the strangely strong stare in the small
eyes amid the folds of crinkled skin.

"Nobody ever tells me what I have to do, feller," Edge countered, and although it was the
truth, the tone of voice in which he spoke the
words made them lack conviction in his own ears.

The old man seemed not to have heard him—or
chose to totally ignore what he said.

"You gotta take care of my old buddy out there.
And not hold against him that he ate part of me.
People have made a meal outta people before,
knowin' what they was doin'. A dumb animal, all
he knows is hunger. And you gotta bury me on
the place. Over to the south side of the clearin'd
be nice. Close to the mine that made me rich to
show I don't hold nothin' against it for killin' me,
and furthest away from the high-nosed folks that
live across the lake. You'll find the tools you need
over at the mine."

He continued to stare fixedly at Edge, the
strength of the gaze undiminished. But his voice
had gradually become fainter. And he seemed
abruptly to realize this, paused to take a deep
breath, and then spoke faster as well as
louder—as if afraid he would not be able to finish
before the will to go on was exhausted.

"After you done that, mister, you work this
claim. You shift that cave-in outta the mine and
you find your reward. And if Ralph or Lee show

up and try to take it away from you, you tell them it was their father's dyin' wish for you to have it. And if they don't take that as the truth, you do what you have to, to protect what's your own."

Again his voice weakened, but his gaze across the room at Edge remained firmly fixed. The half-breed began to roll another cigarette as the stove heat started to warm the chill air of the cabin.

"You look like a man who can manage to do that all right, mister," Barny Galton added.

"What's mine these days ain't much, feller. Most of the time I guess I manage to take care of it."

The dying old man's eyelids began to droop and he complained: "Damnit, the fire's makin' me drowsy, mister. Like to hear you say you'll do like I asked. Before I go?"

He fought to make his eyes as wide as possible and for a stretched second they stared fixedly at Edge again as a match was struck and the cigarette was lit.

The eyelids eased down in front of the eyes and the old man pleaded in a strained whisper "Mister?. . ."

On a stream of tobacco smoke that had only a short and marginal effect on negating the evil stench of the rapidly warming air, the half-breed answered "Bury you, feller. And see if I can find a good home for your dog. No charge."

Galton was unable to get his eyes open again, but he did manage to express a grimace with his mouth. And there was even a degree of venom in his tone when he growled "Then get the hell back on your horse and ride on your way to Lakeview, mister! In all my near eighty-nine years I ain't never took nothin' I didn't pay for—in one way or other! And I ain't gonna start bein' a friggin' panhandler on my friggin' deathbed!"

With his topcoat still on, it was getting to be too hot for Edge beside the stove and he moved to the makeshift table and lowered his rump on to the crates that formed a bench.

"That's right, on your way!" the old man said in a taunting tone as he heard Edge's footfalls on the hard-packed dirt floor. "It'll be the way it was gonna be before you come pokin' your nose in around here! Sayin' you was gonna shoot my dog! Lightin' fires nobody asked you to light! Complainin' about the smell of me I can't help! Why, when I was able bodied I washed up and shaved every day and. — ."

Almost as soon as he began to censure Edge, tears squeezed from under his eyelids and ran across his cheeks. And then the prospect of dying alone, helpless to free the dog from his tether, acted to constrict his throat and choke off the words. His wasted frame started to tremble with silent sobs as the tears flowed faster.

The half-breed sat at the table, quiet and unmoving, sucking every now and then against the cigarette angled from a corner of his mouth. He gazed through the cloud of smoke and out of the smeared window at the blurred scene of the brightly sunlit clearing, pointedly not looking toward the bed where Barny Galton lay weeping in a well of loneliness while he waited to die. But unable to block from his ears the sounds of the old man's ragged breathing.

The cigarette was smoked down to the shortest of butts and Edge allowed the tobacco to burn out just before it was about to singe his lips. Then, perhaps five minutes later, the old man complained:

"Damn you, mister, for not closin' the friggin' door after you!"

Now Edge softly spat out the butt of the cigarette and looked toward the bed to see that Galton was trembling with imagined cold while his face and exposed upper body were beaded with sweat.

"Door's closed, feller. I told you about feeling the cold, didn't I?"

He rose from the crates and started to unbutton his sheepskin coat, intending to go to the bed and drape it over the almost dead man.

"You sonofabitch!" Galton snarled weakly, and managed to crack open his eyes to direct a look of hatred at Edge. "I told you to leave my place, mister! I told you Barny Galton don't take nothin' for nothin'!"

"You and me both, feller," the half-breed said evenly, holding back from approaching the bed.

The old man was too exhausted to maintain high emotion and he began to tremble again. And there was a tremor in his voice as he forced out, "Don't make no sense to me, mister."

"Good chance I could be in much the same kind of spot as you when my time's up, feller. Maybe I figure that if I see you through it, somebody'll be around to—"

"I friggin' told you that unless you take on the claim, I don't—"

"Going to do that, feller."

"What?" This time his lips drew back from his almost toothless gums in a manner to suggest the trace of a smile instead of an unmistakable sneer. And then he started to laugh again. The longest and the loudest yet, as he experienced a simple joy that transcended pain and fear, before the fit of coughing hit him. A racking, uncontrollable paroxysm that shook the man and the bed beneath him.

And set the dog to howling.

For more stretched seconds than seemed possible, the emaciated man in the bed suffered the constant jerking spasms that seemed violent and strong enough to break his bones. And then he died. After he had snapped open his eyes and just for an instant was immobile—gazing at Edge with boundless gratitude. Then a final jerking action attacked his every muscle and he was still for all time. Eyes open, but showing no expression now.

The dog vented a final, very mournful howl, and rose on his hind legs, to put his front paws on the ledge and his snout through the narrow crack at the bottom of the window. He began to whine pitifully. Until Edge came close to the stinking bed and stooped over the corpse, when the animal curled back his lips and growled ominously.

The man looked bleakly at the dog as he closed the death-glazed eyes of Galton and then pulled up the blanket to totally cover the corpse. Said evenly: "It's all right, feller. I ain't going to eat him."

Chapter Three

Just as earlier he had spoken to his gelding to
ease the spooked mind of the horse, so now Edge
talked in a soothing tone to the uneasy German
shepherd.

"He said for you to treat me as a friend, feller.
And I guess you don't find that idea very appealing. Know how you feel. Don't make many myself.
Which, I figure, has to give us at least something
in common."

The dog had stopped growling and was whining softly again as he tried to force the window
open wider with his snout. But it was firmly stuck.

"But before we do much more about develop-
ing our relationship, I have to get the body
buried. So this is what's going to happen next,
feller. I'm going to wrap up the remains in these
bed blankets and carry the whole bundle outside.
Leave it over to the side of the clearing where he
said he wanted to have the grave. Then go find
the mine, bring back a shovel, and do the bury-
ing chore."

The dog had ceased to whine now and dropped

down from the window. Sat below it with his head
cocked first on one side and then the other, listening to the voice of the stranger.

Edge went on, as he stooped over the bed to
free the bottom blanket from under the mattress:
"Between me coming out of the door and reaching the side of the clearing, you'll have a chance
to take a chunk out of me. But I'll have a gun in
my hand and if you try, you won't—"

The dog gave a short, sharp bark which
sounded of impatience.

"All right, I'm not usually this talkative, feller,"
Edge countered, speaking as much for his own
benefit now as he hefted the blanket-wrapped
corpse up from the bed and fought back down his
throat the threat of retching when the most powerful wave of stench yet was released. "Just
wanted you to know how we stand. Kind of like
warning a man not to point a gun at me twice unless he's ready to squeeze the trigger the second
time. You attack me again, you'd better go for the
throat. And get it."

He stood beside the bed with the rancid-smell-
ing body draped over his left shoulder. And grimaced through the window at the dog, which
barked again. Then he turned to go across the
single room of the cabin, eased open the door,
and drew the Frontier Colt from his coat pocket.
Thumbed back the hammer before he used a boot
to draw the door open wider.

The German shepherd was still under the
partly opened window. But was standing now and
moved just his head to follow the slow progress of
Edge, who walked in a shallow arc to go around

the animal. Sideways for a few yards and then backwards, so as to keep watching the dog and aiming the revolver at him.

Except for the inanimate gun, which held no fear for the dog, there was not a trace of aggression in the manner of man or animal. While over on the far side of the clearing, the gelding cropped leisurely at a patch of lush grass beside the start of the trail down from the lakeside promontory.

To the side of the rock outcrop around which Edge had ridden into the clearing, he cautiously lowered his burden to the ground. Still gripping the revolver but no longer constantly watching the silent and unmoving dog, which was now several yards away. Then, because he was specifically looking for it, he easily found a well-trodden way into the timber, which quickly took him out of sight and range of the German shepherd.

It was just a narrow footpath that twisted and turned among the fir trees and intervening brush, all the while dropping down an incline not so steep as the slope that he had ridden up from the shore of the lake. And it ended in a rocky hollow at the base of a low cliff face with a number of holes cut into it—all of them demanding that a man be on hands and knees to enter them. Ten in all along the escarpment, which had trees growing along its rim. Just as there were other trees growing around the horseshoe-shaped curve of the shallow depression at the base of the rock face.

Littering the area outside of several of the adits was a scattering of implements, most of them rusted and broken. Miner's candlesticks and man yokes, picks and shovels, timber props and sections of carts, pails and pans, axes and hammers.

Edge made for where the most serviceable looking of the shovels lay, going down into the hollow and walking over ground made up of small chunks of rock that had been taken from the ten tunnels. And without using time to delve more deeply into the workings of Barny Galton's claim, returned up from the hollow and along the gently rising, twisting, and turning pathway to the clearing.

The dog had now moved from under the cabin window and was lying on his belly, head resting on the blanket-wrapped body of his former master. Silent and looking at Edge with the most doleful of eyes.

"No sweat, feller," the man told the animal. "Unless you ain't fed up with that by the time I get the grave dug."

He started straight in to work on the chore, just a feet feet from where the German shepherd watched him and within easy reach if the animal turned abruptly vicious again. Aware of this danger, he talked as before to the grieving dog—first with the revolver resting still cocked on the ground and then, when the work negated the need for the coat, nestling with the hammer forward in his holster.

"I'm crazy, you know that, feller? I could have been long gone from here. Down that trail from the other side of the place and maybe even arrived in town by now. Having me a drink or eating a meal. With my eye on a woman to share my bed tonight in a hotel where other men are paid to do the chores. And with no damn troubled conscience about not coming back to the place when he called out for help."

He looked long and hard at the dog while he rested for a few moments in the grave that was as wide and long as necessary but only a foot or so deep. Seeing the animal clearly for perhaps the first time. Close to a hundred pounds of lean-built dog, four feet high and half again as long from the base of the tail to the nose. Various shades of brown and gray short hair, with a long and narrow triangle of white on his chest. A finely shaped head with ears fast to prick, eyes that were clear even when they expressed the animal's sadness. And a full set of unbroken and gleaming white teeth—this the only feature of which he had taken much notice before, allied with the powerful bulk of the animal.

So a handsome dog in good health. Which had been well cared for before Barny Galton had his accident. Maybe had been overfed, for he certainly did not look undernourished after so long without any food except for one bizarre meal.

"Instead of which, I'm suddenly in the grave-digging business. With a chance of getting my throat ripped out if you take it into your head to make the try. And if that don't happen, I'm stuck with you unless I can find you a home. Unless he wasn't as crazy as he seemed to be. And there really is a fortune to be made out of his claim. In which case—hell, I'm not joking about being crazy, feller."

This last growled after a yawn caused him to

look toward the dog for the first time in a few minutes. And he saw the animal was now stretched
out on his side with his back to the corpse and the
gravedigger, about to go to sleep.

"I'm almost talking to myself."

He worked faster now, sweating constantly but
not heavily in the bright sunlight of the cool fall
afternoon while his mind remained as empty of
thoughts as his face was vacant of expression. He
had selected a site several feet in from the trees
fringing the clearing and he did not hit any roots.
When the grave was deep enough to accommo-
date him upright to his chest, he called a halt to
the digging and climbed out of the hole.

The dog raised and turned his head to see what
was happening, but made no other move nor any
sound at all as Edge put the corpse into the grave
with as much dignity as was possible, made sure
Barny Galton was put to rest face up. The dog lost
interest and was spread flat out on his side again
during the whole time it took for the displaced
earth to be shoveled back into the hole.

The elongated mound of fresh earth was for the
present a grave marker in itself. But time and na-
ture would eventually camouflage such a sign of
man's mortality. So he used a dozen or so small
rocks, dug from the earth but not put back, to
shape a cross on top of the mound. This symbol,
too, would one day be obliterated. But it was as
much as the man called Edge was prepared to do
in his unaccustomed role of undertaker. And
when he stood up from completing this final
touch, he felt strangely embarrassed in his own
company, as if ashamed of what he had done.

The dog whined softly, like he sensed a darkening of the man's mood and was ready to be sympathetic to it or afraid of it.

Edge shook free of the feeling and as the dog rose on to his haunches, asked of him, "You ready to give that friend stuff a try, feller?"

He dropped on to his haunches and extended a hand, palm uppermost. The dog thrust his head forward and tentatively sniffed the brown-skinned hand. Then licked at the dried sweat of the man's labors. Edge allowed this for a few moments before he began to ruffle the fur on the head of the animal. The dog panted, his breath hot. The man eased slowly upright and stepped closer to the still seated dog, as he reached with his free hand into the hair at the nape of his neck. The dog eyed the open straight razor with the same trusting disinterest as he had earlier viewed the Colt.

All the time this was taking place, Edge talked in the familiar soothing tone, telling the German shepherd that he was a fine dog and describing the kind of meal they would shortly be sharing.

Then he brought the razor toward the head of the dog from the side. And cut through the tether rope just above the knot that was not of the running kind.

"There you go, feller," he said with a note of relief in his voice now as he stepped back from the animal and slid the razor back into its concealed sheath. Added, "If you want to, that is."

The dog looked uncomprehendingly up at the man, in search of but failing to find a word of command that would register. Or maybe a partic-

ular whistle such as Galton had used to bring the
first attempted attack to an end.

"How about eat, feller? You understand eat?
Food? Grub? Chow?"

The animal was obviously concentrating hard.
But gave no response of any kind until, with a
shrug and a short sigh, Edge stooped to retrieve
his topcoat and turned to move away from the
grave. When the dog immediately rose and
moved in close to the man's left leg, tail swaying
and eyes bright as they gazed up in eager search
of approval.

Edge grinned down at the big dog and offered,
"It's a start."

Then, for the next thirty minutes or so, while
Edge prepared and cooked a meal from the diminished supplies in his saddlebags, the dog was
constantly beside him except when he was inside
the cabin which was now warm with stove-heated
air that no longer smelled of the previous owner.
But he never got under the half-breed's feet—was
fast and agile enough to be always out of range
when the man suddenly slowed or changed direction unexpectedly. Almost as if he anticipated the
intentions of his new adopted owner.

Which was disquieting at first. Just as it was
strange to see the dog freeze for a full second or
so outside the doorway each time Edge stepped
over the threshold. Like he was waiting that short
time for the man to change his mind, before he
considered it permissible to sink down on to his
haunches.

But after a while the half-breed accepted simply that the big German shepherd was no more

nor less than an expertly trained animal that needed little more out of life than to give loyalty and obedience to the man who was his master.

Food and drink were among the additional requirements, and the dog drank eagerly when the man refilled his dry bowl at a front corner of the cabin. And ate voraciously from a plate of salt pork and beans that Edge set down just outside the open door. While he ate his share seated on the crate bench at the crate table. A meal that was a combination lunch and supper, for the sun was low beyond the timber-clad ridges in the southwest before it was eaten and dusk was in brief charge of the light while full night hovered ready to stake a not-to-be-denied claim.

Edge rolled a cigarette to smoke with his coffee and as he lit it he experienced an infrequently felt sense of contentment. And yet again the dog seemed to read the mood of the man and matched it. Lay down on his belly with his head between his paws and vented a sigh as he peered through the doorway at the man seated in the rapidly darkening room.

"This is a pretty good place here, feller."

The dog closed his eyes but his ears remained pricked.

"Maybe a better place to rest up than in that town on the other side of the lake."

The dog yawned.

"That's a good idea, I guess. To sleep on it before making any decision." He grinned after taking a swallow of coffee. "Though I figure you've already made yours, far as I'm concerned."

The sleepy canine eyes were briefly opened

again to direct a doleful gaze into the room as the final light of the old day faded.

Edge allowed: "Yeah, you'd rather the poor bastard that died than me. But we've made a pretty good start, wouldn't you say?"

The dog sighed again and then pulled himself wearily up on to his haunches. Bent and turned his head, then raised a hind paw to claw vigorously for several seconds at an itch behind his left ear before he settled down to try again to get to sleep.

When Edge said on a stream of tobacco smoke: "That's right, feller. A damn good start, considering it was from scratch."

Chapter Four

Edge worked on Barny Galton's claim for the next five days, and never once during the waking hours did he fail to be content with what he was doing. He slept long and deeply between sundowns and dawns, untroubled by dreams and nightmares of what had been and what might have been.

What had been was a man alone who rode violent country in a vain search for that which he knew was unattainable. While what might have been was the kind of simple happiness he was now enjoying on this piece of desolate and beautiful Montana terrain.

The War Between the States had started his ride on the violence trail. A war he entered as an Iowa farm boy named Josiah C. Hedges, and finished as a battle-hardened killer, but eager to shed this part of what he had become along with the uniform of a Union cavalry captain.

But events on the small Midwestern farmstead and his reaction to them—dictated by much else that he had become in war—made it impossible

for him to put aside the ways of a killer. For the
crippled kid brother he had left to run the place
while he was away was dead. Mutilated, mur-
dered, and left for buzzard meat out front of the
burning house. Along with Patch, the dog who
had died easier, with just one bullet in him. And
one of the murderers who was himself dead.

There were five more men involved in the killing of young Jamie Hedges and the burning of the
farmstead and its crops. And the elder brother
felt compelled to use all the skills so harshly
learned in war to track down the killers and make
them pay for what they had done. But the country
was at uneasy peace by then and a man who took
the law into his own hands was guilty of stepping
outside the law. And thus did Josiah C. Hedges,
late of the Federal army, become a wanted civil-
ian. And thus did he become the man called
Edge, who, he was convinced for a long time, was
destined by his cruel ruling fates to ride the violence trail as a form of punishment that was
harsher than any the human mind could conceive
and implement.

Never allowed to keep anything he treasured
and doomed to lose, in a welter of spilled blood
and the sound of agonized screams, anyone who
came to mean more to him than a mere passing
face in a crowd.

Self-pity and even an occasional notion of sui-
cide had started to visit his mind then. And anger
at the entire world for the position he was forced
to adopt in it.

But then came too many of the closest kind of
calls with death. Not always on the best of days or

in the most idyllic of places, but invariably the experiences made Edge realize that if life was all he had, then he would do whatever was necessary to keep it. On the dangerous trails he traveled, indulgence in emotion contributed nothing to survival. And could even add to the danger.

This realization altered little in the way he lived the life he was now determined to preserve at all costs against all enemies save old age. Merely made him more alert to potential threats and hardened his attitudes toward his fellow human beings. Which meant he was constantly on his guard in even the most outwardly innocuous surroundings, and that if any man or woman sought to be to him more than that mere passing face in the crowd, he remained emotionally detached.

By living his life this way—decided now that it was by personal choice and not at the whim of some ethereal ruling destiny—he was still on the violence trail, and in surviving the frequent explosions of lethal trouble he sometimes suffered physical pain. But not for a very long time had he experienced more than a twinge of anguish.

Here in Montana at the fall of the year, it would have been easy for a man less resolved to facing a bleak future with indifference to have been tempted to change his philosophy. Or, if not that, to have indulged in self-pity that such a pleasant circumstance could not last for very long.

But during those five days Edge did not once plan beyond the end of whatever chore occupied him. Though the Frontier Colt was always ready in the tied-down holster during the day and the Winchester shared his bedroll at night. And he

never once felt foolish after work or sleep that the
area of the mine and the cabin had remained
peaceful. The German shepherd had never
needed to growl a warning that an intruder was
approaching.

Then, on the evening of the fifth full day at
Barny Galton's claim at the landward end of the
promontory that jutted out into the water of Mirror Lake, there was just enough food left for one
more meal—for the dog.

The old-timer had been almost totally out of
meat when he died and Edge had eked out what
was in his saddlebags to insure the dog had a
meal a day; if not largely of meat, then flavored
with the juices of meat cooked earlier. While for a
day and a half Edge ate from the meager harvest
of the vegetable plot on the north side of the
clearing.

So, after eating a breakfast of beans and feeding the dog a plate of hardtack and sourdough
bread soaked in gravy at the dawning of the sixth
day, Edge took his saddle from a corner of the
sleeping area of the cabin where it had been
stored since that first night and cinched it to the
back of the bay gelding. The German shepherd,
which had been free to roam but had never been
more than a few yards from the man, sat down
close by and thrust his head toward the rising sun
to vent a howl. That was perhaps a more melancholy sound than those he uttered to mark the dying of his former master.

"You're as frigging crazy as I am, you know
that, feller?" the half-breed muttered. "A dog is
supposed to howl at the moon, not the sun. And if

you had the sense to go off and catch yourself a rabbit or squirrel or whatever, I wouldn't need to ride over to Lakeview."

The man had talked to the dog a lot during the preceding days in a variety of different tones of voice, depending upon the location and the progress being made with whatever chore was engaging him. Now, as on all those other occasions, the dog paid close attention to what was being said to him. Gave no indication that he understood anything, but moved off in the wake of the half-breed. And all that was different was that today the man was sitting astride a horse. A change of circumstances not so extreme that the dog failed to remain on guard as he followed the horse and rider across the clearing toward the start of the trail down the east side of the high ground. And, likewise, Edge was not overly concerned with whether the dog should accompany him on the trip to be oblivious to extraneous factors.

And thus did his sharply honed sixth sense for impending menace sound a warning signal in his mind at precisely the same moment that the dog growled.

Which was a moment before a man ordered: "Hold it right there, you lousy claim jumper! Or we'll blow your conniving head right off your shoulders."

They were halfway across the side of the clearing between the front corner of the cabin and the start of the trail, with the vegetable patch in between.

Edge reined in the gelding immediately, just before he was about to steer the horse around the depleted rows of crops. The dog imitated the halting action of the horse in the same way he reacted instantly when following Edge on foot. But he continued to growl softly and ominously with his hackles up and his body tensed for a forward bound.

"Easy, feller," Edge soothed, and this served to quiet the dog just as a man stepped into sight at the top of the trail on the other side of the vegetable patch. A short, thin, sandy-haired man wearing wire-framed spectacles that probably made him look older than he was. So, somewhere between forty-five and fifty-five. Soft looking and dressed in a city-style suit with a caped ulster coat unbuttoned all the way. The suit dark blue and the topcoat cream. He was holding a gray, stiff-brimmed Stetson in his left hand, like he thought it would be more acceptable to kill somebody with the revolver in his right if he were bareheaded.

Fear showed in every plane of his hollow-cheeked, pointed-jawed, gray-and-purple colored face. And in his splay-legged, leaning-forward stance with his gun hand stretched out from his shoulder to the limit.

"Guess you have to be either Ralph or Lee." the half-breed said evenly, his glittering ice blue eyes moving without haste back and forth along the narrow track between their lids in a vain search for somebody else.

"Ralph Galton, damnit!" the frightened man snapped. "But I'll ask the questions—"

"Lee the other one?"

"Lee's my brother, damnit!" The dudishly

dressed man who looked so totally out of place in the Montana timber country seemed to respond automatically to what Edge asked—and then instantly resented what he had done. "And you better do like I said and give me the answers I want!"

"Right at the start you talked about *we*, feller," the half-breed said in the same even tone as before, which contrasted starkly with the nervous excitement of the other man's attitude. "Your pa mentioned there were the two sons and I was wondering if the other one was with you? Hiding, but with you."

A woman said from in the timber to Ralph Galton's right: "Lee ain't no place around here, claim jumper! My husband meant me! But don't you get no idea that I won't back him up if needs be—just because I'm a weak woman!"

She made more noise coming out of her hiding place in the trees than when she went into it. And when the half-breed saw her emerge on to the trail to stand beside her husband, he was briefly intrigued at how she had managed to move so secretively to get so close to the cabin in the clearing.

"This is my wife, Janet," Ralph Galton introduced formally, and seemed to be greatly relieved that she was beside him.

"Ralph, you're a damn fool!" she accused him with a sigh as she continued to glare menacingly at Edge.

She was a match for his five-and-a-half-foot height, but weighed considerably more than he did. Was almost obese, with a build that probably meant she measured the same around her chest, waist, and hips. Her legs, too, were unfemininely over sized. Like her arms. And the garb she wore served to emphasize rather than disguise her bulk—black denim pants and a white silk shirt with the sleeves rolled up to the elbows skin-tight.

Her short neck was circled by a black kerchief knotted on the side and she wore a white Stetson to almost complete an outfit that had probably been purchased far to the east under the impression that it was just what all the women on the frontier were wearing. Only her work-spurred black riding boots looked hardwearing enough to be entirely suitable for the kind of country she was in.

Between hat brim and kerchief she had an extremely pretty face for a woman who was in her forties. Round and smooth skinned, with a flawless cream and pink complexion, big green eyes, and a rosebud mouth. A snub nose and dimpled cheeks. Flanked by ringlets of sheeny black hair.

Also sheeny were the twin barrels of the sawed-off shotgun she aimed at Edge, rock-steady in her fleshy hands.

"You and Ralph both, ma'am," the half-breed said. "For showing up this way and pointing guns at me. After you've stopped doing that, don't ever do it again unless you're ready to fire them. Because I'll sure as hell be doing my best to kill you. Give folks the one warning if I'm able. Name's Edge."

He looked from one to the other and back again while he spoke, nodding to each in turn after introducing himself. Saw that his soft-spoken words had expanded the fear of the man with the .44

Tranter, while the woman with the twin-barrel Purdy shotgun was driven into a deeper rage, which left her speechless for a second or so when he was through.

In which time Edge tapped his heels to the flanks of the gelding and started to make his farewells with a touch of his left index finger to the brim of his hat.

"Place is all yours now. You'll see where I buried—"

"Just a goddamn minute there!" Ralph Galton blurted. And dropped his hat so that he could bring up the hand to help the other one steady the wavering aim of the revolver.

"You ain't goin' no place until you explain to us—oh, my God!"

The woman wrenched her head to the side, to peer into the brush among the trees. And dragged the shotgun around to aim at something that brought her to the same degree of fear that her husband was experiencing.

The cause of the abrupt and drastic change in Janet Galton was a low but highly threatening animal growl.

Despite being certain of which animal made the sound, Edge felt compelled to look down, to the side and rear of where he sat the gelding. He rasped, "Doggone."

Chapter Five

The half-breed had been so used to having the German shepherd almost as close to him as his shadow during the days at the claim, that he was as surprised as the Galtons when the animal announced his presence in the timber.

First he was angry at himself for not having seen the dog move stealthily away, under cover of the crops and then the brush among the trees. In the next instant felt something akin to pride in the dog for his cunning and intelligent initiative. Next, fear for the life of the animal.

All this in a part of a second. With no time to question why he felt these compassionate emotional responses from a store that was supposed to be devoid of them, he reacted physically to the dictates of instinct—in the same way as if it were his life that was threatened.

He jerked the Winchester out of the scabbard with his right hand. And needed simply to thumb back the hammer because there was already a bullet in the breech. This as he brought the rifle up to his shoulder and his left hand moved in a blur of speed across his body to grip the barrel.

The range was about fifty feet across the vegetable patch and, because he was astride the gelding, the trajectory was downward, more so than if his target was the fat woman or her husband. Instead, it was the Purdy, which was already canted at an angle to locate the dog but was not yet swung on to the target.

Edge squeezed the trigger of the rifle.

Janet Galton shrieked in terror and perhaps some pain as the shotgun jerked in her hands, violently moved by the impact of the Winchester's bullet hitting the tops of the barrels about three inches back from the muzzles.

The gun slammed hard against the ground. The dull thud of the ricochet penetrating a tree trunk preceded, by part of a second, the crack of Ralph Galton's revolver. The bullet went low and wide to explode rock splinters from the outcrop at the far corner of the clearing.

Edge worked the lever action of the Winchester and raked the rifle to the side to align the sights on the thick torso of the woman. This as her husband used both thumbs to cock the Tranter; but the hammer was stiff and the barrel tilted toward the sky that was brightening with the light of the just-rising sun.

The dog continued to growl.

"Tell you people like it is," Edge said, his tone of voice the same as before the exchange of gunfire. And perhaps this served better than a commanding snarl to capture the attention of the physically ill-matched couple at the start of the trail. "The lady don't break open the gun and empty out the cartridges, I'll kill her where she stands. You feller, you ease the hammer of the revolver forward and you put the thing away. If you don't do that, it'll be another fatal mistake."

"What about this damn dog?" the woman asked huskily while her husband was struggling to swallow the constricting fear in his throat.

"Why would I want to kill him, ma'am?"

"Call him off, damnit!"

"Janet, do like he tells you!" Ralph blurted. And did not follow the instructions Edge had given him. Instead, released his grip on the revolver with one hand and with the other hurled the Tranter off into the timber at his side of the trail.

Janet Galton looked from the German shepherd to Edge and back again. The fear mixed with anger gradually ebbed from her round and pretty face, to be replaced by a brand of defiance in defeat. But then she did as her husband urged—directing a fixed, sneering look at the half-breed as she broke open the shotgun and extracted the cartridges by feel. She pushed them into a pocket of her shirt and lodged the broken-open Purdy in the crook of an arm as she challenged:

"Just to ease Ralph's mind, claim jumper. He worries about me and that gives him acid in the stomach. I think you and your mutt are both the same—all damn noise."

Edge had already eased the hammer of the rifle to the rest and replaced it in its scabbard. Now took up the reins and heeled the gelding into an easy walk around the vegetable patch.

"Easy, feller," he said to silence the growling dog just before he halted his mount on the trail, ten feet from where the Galtons stood: the husband still afraid and the wife continuing to wear the challenging look. The dog circled back out of the timber and came to sit on his haunches beside the gelding's left hind leg.

"Now what, big talker?" the woman sneered.

"Janet, don't provoke him!" her husband urged. "You'll have to excuse Janet, Mr. Edge. See, I got this letter from my father telling how he'd struck it rich on his claim. About how he was old and wanted to see his sons before he passed away. Hoping that by bringing us together—Lee and me—and sharing the inheritance between us, we'd forget our differences and be friends. Well, Janet and me, we near run ourselves ragged making fast time out here to Montana Territory from Buffalo, New York State, and I guess Janet just couldn't take any more without blowing her—"

"Shut up, you damn fool!" his wife cut in after listening with mounting impatience to his spluttering explanation. "Sure, I'm ready to blow up! On account of you makin' such a hash of this. If it had been you the mutt looked like settin' on and that guy took a shot at you, I wouldn't have missed blowin' him outta his damn saddle!"

"Ma'am," Edge put in.

And drew both their attentions back to him after they had glowered at each other.

"What?" the woman snapped.

"What you think of your husband is of even less interest to me that what you think of me. Now do you want to listen to what I started to tell you? Or do you want to spend a lot of time fretting that you didn't?"

Janet snorted in the kind of tone that suggested it was as close as she ever came to voicing an obscenity.

Ralph Galton, his nervousness reduced in direct proportion to how irritation with his wife expanded, said: "We left the buggy at the foot of the hill when we saw your fire smoke, Mr. Edge. If Janet will not do as you ask, I'll be glad to pay attention to you while we go down to the lakeshore."

He stooped, retrieved his hat, and jammed it on his head with a determined gesture.

"Spit it out, claim jumper!" the fat woman commanded.

Tersely, the half-breed related the relevant events since his arrival in the area of Barny Galton's claim. The man remained attentive and the woman skeptical, except when he mentioned the dog being fed a human leg—which spread grimaces of revulsion across the faces of both. When he was through, the son of the dead miner said:

"I appreciate you doing what my father asked, Mr. Edge."

"I'll want to see the old skinflint dug up to make sure he died that way before I'll believe—"

"You can't miss the grave, ma'am," Edge interrupted evenly and heeled the horse forward, so that they had to step to either side of the trail to let him pass.

The dog instantly followed the gelding.

Ralph continued to harbor anger for his wife's

resolute determination to keep doubting the half-breed's story. While she seemed to be searching her mind for other bases of suspicion. Did not find one until horse, rider, and dog had gone by.

Then: "And you expect me to believe you're ready to just ride on out of here? After all those hours of grubbing in the mine and coming up empty handed? Not in a million years, mister. Either you found what brought Ralph and me all the way from Buffalo and you're taking off with it. Or you plan to come on back and take it off Ralph and me when—"

"Woman, he was already leaving before we showed up!"

"So all right, he's got it already. And if we let him ride away from here this whole damn trip out to the lousy West has been wasted, Ralph!"

"Well, I believe him! If it wasn't true what he said, why didn't he just shoot us down when he had that rifle covering us?"

"Because it's like I said! Him and his mutt are both the same! Make a lot of threatening sounds, but that's as far as it goes!"

"Yet you're saying he killed my father and—"

"So maybe that part of what he says is true, Ralph! But if you was told there was a fortune on the claim and worked your fingers to the bone to get at it, would you give up and be on your way just because somebody else showed up and . . ."

Edge had been riding steadily down the curving slope of the trail toward the lake, unable to avoid overhearing the shouted exchange between the husband and wife. But gradually their voices dropped and this, in combination with the

thickness of the band of trees intervening, acted
to muffle and eventually totally mask the words.

The half-breed had rolled a cigarette as he
rode down the slope and when the only sounds to
be heard were those made by himself, the horse,
and the dog, he lit it, as if in celebration of being
this far away from the squabbling couple. Then
he glanced down at the big German shepherd
strolling alongside the rear of the horse and said:
"Much obliged, feller. Know I'd have killed them
if needs be, but what about you?"

The dog glanced up at him with noncompre-
hension.

"Know how to call you off and what to say to get
you to attack me. How do I get you to do more
than snarl at other people?'

The animal continued to pay concentrated attention to the man astride the horse, ears pricked
and eyes appealing for a command that could be
understood by a canine mind.

"Kill—get him—go, boy—take him?" Edge
tried and drew no response. Then he shrugged
and faced front as he growled: "Hell, what does it
matter? Soon as wer reach Lakeview I'll get you
fixed up with some nice family and go back to taking care of myself."

The dog whined softly, and when Edge looked
down at him again it was to see him with his head
drooping, ears laid back flat, and eyes filled with
accusing disapproval.

"For a dumb animal," the half-breed counter-
accused, "you sure do have a lot to say for yourself. When it suits you."

The dog made no further sound and when, a

few moments later, Edge glanced at him again, he was strolling with his tail swaying, his head held high, ears erect, and eyes bright, and with his jaws open a little, like he was grinning.

Edge faced front and rasped "Sonofabitch!" Then showed a broad grin of his own that even injected some warmth into the blueness of his eyes as he added, "Ain't that the accursed truth, feller?"

Chapter Six

Man, horse, and dog had come down this slope often during the past five days, to drink and for the half-breed to bring fresh water from the lake back to the cabin in the clearing. This cold, brightly sunlit morning the German shepherd gave a low growl of nervous suspicion at the unfamiliar sight of a buggy with a black mare in the traces that was parked at the point where the trail started to rise from the lakeshore.

The rig was a canopy-topped country wagon that had seen better days. But not on the long trails from Buffalo to Mirror Lake. For on the rear was a large trunk decorated with a number of transportation company tags, which showed the Galtons had sailed aboard a clipper from Boston to San Francisco, then ridden the train to Salt Wells, Wyoming. From there the trunk had been shipped up to Lakeview by the Great Northern Freight Company.

Edge saw the tags as he rode around the stalled rig, the dog quiet again in the wake of the easy, walking horse. And, as he continued along the trail that took him in the wrong direction for a mile to get around the arm of water curving south, he felt a mild stab of resentment toward Ralph and Janet Galton. Who had made such an arduous trip to bring to an end one of the most contented periods of his life he could ever recall.

No, he corrected himself in his free-ranging mind. Not bringing his time at the claim to an end as such, rather, being responsible for him leaving after so short a time. For eventually he would have left the place of his own volition, when the grueling labor of shifting debris from the caved-in mine ceased as a challenge and became a bore, or forced back into the outside world by the need to raise eating money after his stake was gone before he got to the reward of which the dying old man had spoken.

"But never mind, uh feller," he said to the dog as they rounded the end of the narrow stretch of water and started north. "All good things have to come to an end. And I guess it's better they do before they turn bad."

The big German shepherd gave a short and noncommittal bark. And the half-breed muttered:

"Shit, I really have to stop talking to you like I figure you know what I'm saying!"

Another, more determined bark, seemed to take the man mildly to task. So Edge countered:

"And you got to quit making like you do know what I'm saying."

Then the man and dog took to concentrating entirely on watching the surrounding country as the trail turned away from the shore of the lake and rose up another timbered slope. At the top it ceased to be an exclusive route to and from the claim of the late Barny Galton, for it intersected with a broader, much more heavily used trail that angled up from the southeast.

At the start of the way to the claim, an ancient and leaning sign proclaimed, in lettering seared with branding irons into the timber crossmember, PRIVATE PROPERTY—NO STRANGERS ALLOWED.

Edge steered his mount into a left turn to follow the wider trail toward Lakeview, allowing the gelding to select the precise course between the wheel ruts of heavily laden wagons and across the countless hoofprints of other horses—the impressions left in the mud after heavy rain and baked by later sun.

There was little to see save for trees and brush to either side, the pocked trail below, and the smooth, blue sky above, with just an occasional glimpse of a small section of Mirror Lake to the left. But already on this bright, cool morning the innocently beautiful treescape had unleashed the threat of death and thus was the half-breed's habitual watchfulness from behind an attitude of outward ease, just a little more wary than usual. Sufficiently so for the German shepherd to sense the man's inner tension and to maintain a more intense surveillance over his surroundings than was normal for the animal.

But the peace of the forest remained undisturbed beyond the sounds of its rightful inhabitants going about their daily business of survival, and those made by the intruders on the trail as they drew closer to the lakeside town that rider and mount should have reached almost a week previously.

The trail that connected Lakeview with the outside world stayed above the level of the water and in the timber until it curved westward, when it dipped suddenly and emerged from the trees to run directly alongside the shingle beach for the rest of the way into town.

The timber-built town, which owed its existence to timber, comprised the waterfront streets and another which paralleled it three blocks north, and four side streets connecting the main, broader ones.

At the town marker, which claimed Lakeview was two thousand feet above sea level and had a population of one thousand souls, the trail forked, the more heavily traveled section angling to become the main inland street while the other branch led on to the thoroughfare that followed the shore.

Edge went this way as he struck a match on the Winchester stock to light a freshly rolled cigarette. He was able to see around the curving, half-mile length of the street that it was primarily residential in character. Single-, two-, and, occasionally, three-story houses were aligned behind picket fences on the north side. Each with front-window views across the street, the piers with the tied-up rowboats and the lake to the timber-clad heights beyond.

At the end of the street to the east was a steepled church. Midway along a meeting hall. A schoolhouse was at the western end. All the structures frame built with steeply pitched roofs. All were well maintained and scrupulously clean—the fence-enclosed yards of the houses as well tended as the cemetery beside the church.

There was nobody on the street at this mid-morning hour. But here and there a woman was at work on a flower bed or engaged in an outside window-cleaning chore. And to those who looked at him, he tipped his hat and drew responses of either a smile or a cheerful greeting.

None of the waterfront houses bore a sign to suggest it accepted boarders, and so Edge turned his mount up the final cross street, which was no different from the others he had ridden by. Residential again, but flanked by smaller, less well cared for houses. All of just single story and built directly on to the street without benefit of front yards. And with no fences to mark a property line across the ample space between them.

An old man with a blanket over his shoulders and another wrapped around his legs sat in the open doorway of an east-facing shack, getting a little warmth from the morning sun as he smoked a pipe and drank something from a tin mug. He showed more frowning interest in the German shepherd than in Edge, until he nodded and took the pipe from between his discolored teeth. And said as the half-breed rode level with him, "I'd say that there dog is the one that crazy old coot Barny Galton had one time."

"You'd be right to say it, feller," Edge confirmed.

The old man took a mouthful of whatever was in the mug, turned his head to the side, and spat it out. Then said, "Fortune my ass, the crazy old coot!"

"Don't use bad language, Pa," a woman complained in a long-suffering tone from inside the house. "And what's the use me gettin' you medicine from the doc if you keep on spittin' it into the street?"

"It tastes like what I go to the privy to get rid of, Lydia." He took another mouthful and spat this out more forcefully. Added in a louder voice, "Reckon it's what the doc goes to his privy to get rid of."

"You'll die, you don't let me look after you, Pa!"

"I'll die anyway, Lydia!"

Just as had happened on the fringe of the claim on the far side of Mirror Lake, Edge rode out of earshot of the exchange between the concerned Lydia and her sour-tempered father. Heard as a final comment, spoken in a tone of curiosity:

"Wonder how that feller got the dog away from that crazy-as-a-coot Barny Galton? Fortune, my ass!"

Then the half-breed reined in his horse at the point where the side street joined Lakeview's commercial thoroughfare, which was more in keeping with the cross streets than the town's lake frontage.

Inevitably, the buildings were of timber, unpainted or painted a long time ago and never refurbished. A mixture of single- and two-story buildings, with sidewalks or individual stoops out front of most of them. Weathered signs along awnings or hung from brackets named the busi-

nesses engaged in behind each neglected facade.

Stores supplying essentials and luxuries. A
bank and a newspaper. A saloon and a livery stable. A doctor's office and one used by an attor-
ney. A sheriff's office and a stage-line depot. A
horse and wagon hire outfit. A clock repairer and
a gunsmith. A blacksmith and a barber. A dentist
and a hotel.

None of the commercial premises were very
big and they were squeezed close together in a
number of varying styles—as if new businesses
were introduced to Lakeview over a lengthy period and nobody wanted to set up shop outside of
the original eastern and western limits of the
street.

From the western extremity of the street, a final
block along from where Edge sat his gelding to
take stock of the town, a trail headed out into the
timber. And snaked toward an area he had seen
from a distance as he approached the far side of
town—and which had told him the reason for
Lakeview being here. Out there, behind the high
ground that fringed the lake, was a massive and
ugly scar on the Montana landscape. A vast area
of rolling hills that had been stripped of its timber
and showed up as an obscene, dark-hued patch
of now barren land encircled by the lush green
foliage of the coniferous Douglas firs which were
yet to be felled.

At the center of the timber-ravaged area was a
sawmill that belched smoke from four stacks. A
plant that was, even from a distance of two miles,
very much a part of the town in at least one

way—in that it had previously been small at the start and was added to as the lumber business boomed.

"Hey, mister, ain't that Old Man Galton's dog you got there?" a boy of about sixteen asked as he crossed from one corner of the side street to the other with a heavy-looking sack on a shoulder. He took a wide sweep out into the center of the main street, apparently afraid to get close to the German shepherd, who sat quietly on his haunches at his accustomed position beside the left hind leg of the gelding.

"Guess there ain't many like him around here, kid?" the half-breed replied as he dropped the cigarette butt to the street.

"Don't reckon there's another one like him in the whole damn territory," the boy answered. "Didn't the old-timer tell you to always keep him on a leash?"

Edge shook his head and heeled the horse forward and into a right turn along the center of the commercial street, which was quiet compared to the activity around the distant sawmill and a felling area to the west of it.

The boy with the sack was startled by the abrupt way in which the dog moved to follow the gelding. And he leaped up on to the sidewalk to lunge in through the doorway of a meat market.

There were women shoppers and a few men past work age idling their time on the sidewalks. And without exception they looked at the stranger in town—as often as not did a double take to assure themselves that they really were seeing the obviously familiar German shepherd accompanying the horseman. But none of these people commented on the dog.

It was not yet within thirty minutes of noon and although Edge made it a rule never to drink hard liquor until after midday, he reined the gelding to a halt out front of the Treasure House Saloon and swung down from the saddle to hitch him to the rail. Then sat on the sidewalk with his booted feet on the street and appeared to be indifferent to everything except the dog who sat beside him—stroked his head from time to time but more often gazed into the middle distance at whatever images his mind chose to conjure.

But, as always, he was aware of what was happening around him, conscious of people passing by on the opposite sidewalk and moving in back of him on this one. And he sensed the various feelings they had about him, which ranged from intrigued curiosity to something close to resentment.

Then, when the clock above the stoop of the clock repairer's showed the time at just five minutes to noon and he was about to rise from his seat on the sidewalk, he knew he was about to be approached for an explanation. And so he stayed where he was, ready to answer any reasonable questions the short, pudgy, duster-coated lawman might care to put to him.

But then, from way down at the eastern end of the street, a man yelled, "Stage's comin' in!" and the sheriff altered his direction, quickening his pace along a less acute diagonal to bring him to the front of the Northern Stage Line depot.

A lot of other people converged just as eagerly

on the same spot. And above the noise of the activity, the sheriff tossed over his fleshy shoulder,

"Have a word later, stranger!"

Just as had happened with every other Lakeview citizen so far, the lawman paid more attention to the quietly alert dog than to Edge, who now rose from the sidewalk nodding an acknowledgment that he had heard the request.

The German shepherd rose, too, and was close on the heels of the half-breed in crossing the sidewalk and pushing through the slatted batwing doors. The doors flapped closed behind the man and the animal and a voice snarled in a tone of shocked anger:

"What the hell's the idea, comin' in here with that mutt?"

"So I can have a drink," Edge answered evenly as the clattering sounds of the approaching stage carried into the saloon.

It was a fifty-by-thirty room, deeper than it was wide, with a curving bar counter across the rear left corner. There were ten tables, each ringed by four chairs placed so that there was an aisle between them and the wall by which to reach the bar. A stairway with a rope for a banister canted steeply up the rear wall from near the end of the bar. Daylight from the frosted front window and the doorway decreased to gloom before it reached the rear of the place.

A tall, bulkily built bartender stood behind the bar and a frail-looking woman sat on a high stool with a low back in the space between the bar's end and the start of the stairway.

"Be happy to sell you as many drinks as you

want, stranger," the bartender said, anger expanding as the half-breed and the dog came toward him. Edge unbuttoning the sheepskin coat while the German shepherd growled softly in response to the aggression. "Just as soon as you get that dog outta here!"

"Need a drink to improve the way I feel, feller. Whether you're happy or not doesn't make any difference to me."

He was three-quarters of the way to the bar now and close enough to see that the big bartender was about thirty with clean-cut good looks under a shot of curly red hair. He had the pale complexion of a man who worked inside and took few of his pleasures out in the open air.

Likewise, the woman had a wan look to her appealing face framed by long, straight hair that was redder than the man's. She had blue eyes that appeared disproportionately large, which surveyed the world with a cynicism that was sad in somebody who was just past twenty years old.

He was dressed for this trade in a shirt and pants and a leather bib apron. She for hers in a red dress cut low enough to display the upper slopes of her small breasts and with a slit in the side so that one slender leg encased in fishnet was on show from ankle to mid-thigh.

"Hey, that's real funny, Leo," the woman said nasally and drew back her thin lips to show a false grin.

"What you see me doin' ain't laughin', Rita," Leo muttered in a voice that rasped.

He reached under the bar top and brought out an old, single-shot Spencer carbine. He clicked back the hammer as he rested his elbows on the top of the bar and pressed his cheek to the stock of the gun. To aim at the still softly growling dog, who had immediately sat down when Edge halted at sight of the Spencer.

"Leo's right, lady," the half-breed said evenly, his coat fully unbuttoned now. "Laughing he ain't. But you wouldn't expect that of a man getting ready to die." He reached down to stroke the side of the dog's head and soothed, "Easy, feller."

"Uh?" she countered, and after squinting at the newcomer silhouetted against the light, she quickly shed her attitude of worldly cynicism and opened her mouth to say something as she slid off the stool. Suddenly frightened.

"I'll shoot him sure as—"

"Don't mess with this guy, Leo!" Rita cut in.

"You got just the one bullet in that carbine, feller," Edge said, and now his tone had hardened. Enough to cause Leo's eyes to shift from the quietly seated German shepherd to meet and be trapped by the half-breed's ice-cold gaze. "I got a six-gun here." He gently eased open the right side of his coat to display the Frontier Colt in the holster. Let the coat fall back again before he went on: "You shoot this animal, you'll feel every one of the six slugs going into your hide. And you'll live a long time and feel a lot of pain afterwards."

Leo grimaced in derision, but sweat beads of tension stood out on his forehead and along his upper lip.

"He means it!" Rita urged.

"Rules is rules and I don't allow no animals in—

"There are exceptions to every rule, feller."

"And we got the law in this town!" This said with greater confidence. "Killers don't get away with it in Lakeview!"

"Ain't that what I just said, feller? Since I happen to be in Lakeview right now."

"Damnit, it's only a mutt!"

"I like him a whole lot better than I like you. You want to put the carbine back where you got it and sell me a shot of rye whisky now?"

He restarted his slow walk to the bar as he spoke and the German shepherd was instantly at his heel. Moving out from under the threat of the Spencer, which was not really a threat, since the eyes of the man holding the gun continued to be held by the glittering gaze of Edge.

Outside, the incoming stage had been pulled to a stop at the depot and there was a great deal of shouting between the crew and passengers and the Lakeview citizens who had gone to meet it. Everybody sounded reasonably happy.

Leo was irritable as he straightened up, raising the Spencer and turning it. He clicked the hammer forward before he put the carbine back below the bar top. And growled as he took a bottle and a shot glass off a shelf along the wall behind him: "What if I get a crowd in here? I know dogs. Always in the way. Sprawled out under people's feet all the time. Where's he gonna park his flea-bitten carcass?"

Leo kept nodding across the bar top as he spoke and poured the drink. Unable to see the dog who had sat down again, between the bar front and Edge's legs.

The half-breed glanced down at the animal, picked up his drink and took it at a swallow, set the glass on the bar top for a refill, and told the sour faced bartender, "Guess a dog as big as this one parks his ass wherever the hell he likes!"

The glass was just half refilled when Leo halted the pouring process to demand, "You got the money to pay for what you're havin', stranger?"

Edge pulled aside his coat again and Leo flinched back as Rita caught her breath. But the brown-skinned hand reached into a hip pocket to bring out a roll of bills. A five was peeled off and placed beside the half-filled glass and the roll returned to the pocket.

"Just my stock for sale, not the saloon, moneybags," Leo muttered resentfully as he now filled the glass. "You want any more or will I make change?"

"Change, feller," Edge told him and lifted the glass, but did not drink until he had accepted the change from the five and gone to sit at a table in the corner almost under the canting stairway. His back into the angle of the walls so that he was facing across the saloon. The German shepherd sat at his side and then lay down, head between it its front paws, when the half-breed rolled and lit a cigarette. The rye was taken in small amounts, like it was the best Kentucky sipping whisky.

All this while Leo stared sourly down the length of his saloon at the batwing doors, like he was willing more customers to come through them. And Rita shot a series of surreptitious glances through the open steps of the stairs at the man at the corner table. Then, after asking for a beer she did not pay for and taking a long swallow, she found the courage to slide off her stool and move to lean seductively against the newel at the foot of the stairway. With a smile that was in imminent danger of cracking under the strain of her nervous eagerness, she said:

"Ain't just Leo's stock for sale in the Treasure House, handsome. And I reckon from what I saw you can afford to buy the very best kind of merchandise I got available."

Edge shifted his level gaze from the sheriff, who was coming through the batwing doors, to the whore, who was expertly displaying her legs and breasts to the best immodest effect.

"Obliged, lady, but I guess I'll stay with what I have."

Her smile bagan to transform into a frown as she questioned, "Uh?"

"Don't they say that dog's a man's best friend?"

"You lost me, stranger." The frown had become a scowl.

Edge nodded. "I hope so, lady. Because right now I got no need of a pussy."

Chapter Seven

Leo leaned his head to direct a gust of sardonic laughter at the smoke-stained ceiling of the saloon and then yelled in a bad imitation of the whore's nasal tones: "Hey, that's real funny, Rita! What's a man with a dog want with a pussy!"

"Shut your rotten mouth, Leo!" she shrieked at him and whirled to hurl the glass at the wall. Where it smashed and sprayed beer, in no danger of harming the bartender, Edge, or the sheriff. Then she started up the stairway, and paused to snarl at the half-breed, "I heard that some of you hard as nails, tough-talkin' bastards ain't got what's needed in the sack!"

She clattered on up to the top of the stairs, where she wrenched open a door and slammed it violently closed behind her.

The lawman said wearily as he reached the bar, "Give me a beer, Leo." And as it was being drawn, he glanced up the stairway and added, "That girl ain't never gonna make it as a whore unless she learns to take no for an answer without flyin' off the handle."

Leo scowled up the stairway as he asked, "On the tab, Mr. Herman?"

"On the tab, Leo," the sheriff agreed as he turned to bring his beer toward the table where Edge sat. And asked, "Okay to have that word now?"

The half-breed gestured for him to sit down opposite, which he did and took a sip at his beer before saying:

"Sheriff Herman, the law in Lakeview and Mirror Lake County."

"Edge. Just passing through your jurisdiction, sheriff."

His drink was finished now and he dropped his cigarette butt in the glass so that it sizzled out in the moisture there.

The lawman took another swig of beer. He was more than fifty and maybe closer to sixty. Less than five-feet-six-inches tall with a build and fleshy face that were silent witnesses to an easy and comfortable way of life. But there was something about the set of the lips beneath his bushy black moustache and in the brightness of his green eyes that suggested he would not be found wanting in a suddenly difficult and uncomfortable situation.

His gray duster was open now to show that his jacket, shirt, and pants were as Western in style as his hat. All his clothing gray in color, spotlessly clean but unfancy. Like his gunbelt with an Army Model .44 Remington in the tied-down holster.

"Ain't one for beatin' about the bush, Mr. Edge."

The half-breed nodded his approval of this.

"That there dog is the one Barny Galton used to bring to town on the few occasions he ever hoofed it around the lake?"

"It was Galton's dog, sheriff."

Herman leaned to the side to direct a doubtful look down at the quiet German shepherd, who seemed to be on the verge of sleep.

"Never did trust him much, the way he was always growlin' at folks."

"The dog, Sherriff?"

Herman abruptly emphasized the hard set of his mouth and brightened the harsh light in his eyes as he snapped, "Don't try to be funny at my expense, Edge!"

"This is costing you nothing but time, sheriff. Maybe too much for a man who claims he doesn't beat about—"

"Okay!" Herman cut in, a little chastened by the deserved rebuke. "Last night one of Old Man Galton's sons and his wife reached town on a freight wagon. In too much of a hurry to wait for the stage that would've been a whole lot more comfortable. And in too much of a rush to wait until today to get around to the old man's claim across the lake. So they rented one of Ephraim Browning's rigs and took off in the dead of night. City folks from the East out in this kinda country —hell, shit!"

He paused briefly to drink some more beer and then immediately continued.

"Anyways, that Ralph and Janet Galton roll off into the night and then this mornin' you ride into town with Barny Galton's dog. But that ain't coin-

cidence enough. When the stage reaches Lakeview just a few minutes ago, who's one of the passengers? Lee—Old Man Galton's other son
—that's who. And he wants to know more or less
just what them other Galtons did. Where's his
pa's claim and where he can rent a horse to get to
it."

"You don't say, Mr. Herman," Leo put in, intrigued.

"I do say!" the lawman snapped at the bartender, but then looked back at Edge to growl:
"But I'm sayin' it to you, Mr. Edge. And I'd appreciate hearin' more than smart talk from you. Because Barny Galton's claim is on my patch of territory and if somethin' untoward is goin' on out
there, I should know about it."

There was the click of the latch of a cautiously
opened door on the landing at the top of the stairway. And a floorboard creaked in back of the bar
counter when Leo moved as close to the occupied
table as he could get without lifting the flap and
coming through.

None of which was lost on the sheriff, who said
with a scowl, "If this is goin' to be strictly law
business, we can step across the street to my office, Mr. Edge."

"Nothing I'm ashamed to tell."

Herman leaned forward, like he was encourag-
ing Edge to speak softly, and invited, "So tell it."

The half-breed did so, speaking at a normal
conversational level that was heard by the bartender and the whore. And both of them admitted
this with gasps when he made dispassionate mention of Barny Galton feeding his severed leg to

the dog. He told of the events at the claim almost word for word in the same way he had related them to the Galtons. And added in equally laconic fashion the basic details of the trouble he had with the frightened Ralph and his bellicose wife.

From far to the west of Lakeview, a steam whistle shrilled to end the short silence that followed Edge's telling of what had happened since he reached the south shore of Mirror Lake.

"Lunch break out at lumber camps," the lawman said absently as he gazed into the middle distance and toyed with one side of his moustache as he contemplated what he had been told.

"Poor old bastard," Leo muttered. "What a lousy way to go."

"And everyone figured it was a timber wolf doin' all that howlin' at night last week," the whore contributed sadly from the head of the stairs.

Sheriff Herman brought his mind back to the here and now, made to finish his beer, but decided he could not manage it. He stood up and nodded to the half-breed: "Appreciate your cooperation, Mr. Edge. But you'll understand that I'll need to ride around to the claim to check out a few facts. And until I've done that, it'll be necessary for you to stay in town."

"The hotel the only place a stranger can bed down, sheriff?"

"Yeah. Though I don't know how Max and Polly Webster will feel about the dog."

"Guess I'll go find out."

The lawman went through the batwing doors

and Edge had risen from the table and moved to the threshold of the saloon before the doors had stopped swinging, the German shepherd as close to him as always.

"Damnit, mister, how can you stand to have that creature with you all the time?" the whore asked with a grimace of revulsion as she came down the stairway. "Knowin' he's eaten human flesh!"

Edge hooked a hand over one of the doors to steady it and glanced back at the woman in the revealing dress as she reached the foot of the stairway and climbed on to the stool. And drawled: "Figure he'll be all right with me, Rita. But maybe you should be careful."

"Me—why me?" she demanded as she wrapped both her hands around the fresh glass of beer Leo had drawn for her.

"You're all done up like a dog's dinner."

Chapter Eight

The batwing doors flapped noisily behind Edge and the dog as Leo yelled, "Hey, that's really funny!"

The whore snarled against the bartender's gust of raucous laughter, "Shut your rotten mouth, Leo."

Edge unhitched the gelding from the rail out front of the saloon and led him by the reins toward the hotel, which was two blocks along on the same side of the street. Squeezed between the stage-line depot and Browning's Rentals, and called The Webster House.

The street was busier now, with the first of the men from the lumber camps to reach town, and with children, some escorted by their mothers, out from school for the lunch recess all eager to eat or drink. The team that had hauled the ancient Concord to Lakeview was being taken from the traces by a man who looked like the depot manager while the stage crew held on to and softly cursed at a quartet of fresh and skittish horses. Four passengers waited to board. A man

with a sand-colored beard led a gray gelding
from the premises of Ephraim Browning,
mounted him with difficulty, and rode tentatively
along the street to leave town by the east trail.

Almost everyone was too intent upon what
occupied them to cast more than a passing glance
at the stranger leading his horse and followed by
a dog. Except for the bearded rider, who, when
he felt secure astride his unfamiliar mount, shot
a look over his shoulder. Deeply curious for
stretched seconds until, over a constantly widening range, the slitted blue eyes of Edge locked
with his round, dark ones—when he became suddenly nervous and snapped his head around to
face the way he was going.

"Guess that's Lee Galton?" the half-breed
asked of Herman as the sheriff appeared on the
threshold of Ephraim Browning's premises as he
drew level with the entrance.

"Right, Mr. Edge. Told him briefly what you
told me. Asked him to light a signal fire on the
point across the lake if he thinks the law's needed
over there. Like I say, there's facts needed to be
checked out. But no sense two men ridin' the
same trail for the same reason."

Edge nodded and continued on to the hotel
next door, where he hitched the gelding and
stepped up on the stoop. The travel-weary team
had been taken out of the traces by now and the
fresh horses were being hitched to the stage
across the mouth of the alley that separated the
hotel from the depot. One of the skittish animals
at the front snorted and reared high.

The younger of the two-man crew snarled,

"Get that friggin' dog outta sight, Mex!"

The German shepherd growled and his back hair bristled in response to the tone of aggression in the voice of the man struggling to calm the horse.

Edge turned and came down off the stoop. Stroked the dog's ears and said, "Easy, feller." Then went around his hitched horse and across the mouth of the alley to where the team animal was becoming more agitated. The man trying to control him was cursing louder and more obscenely.

"John!" the older man yelled in a warning tone, moving up to try his hand at bringing the nervous horse under control.

John thought there was no more to the act than his partner coming to his aid in the matter of the hard-to-handle horse. Until he saw the look on the older man's face. But by then it was too late. And even as he swung his head around while still clinging to the long rein of the troublesome horse, a hand hooked over his coat collar at the nape of his neck. To drag him violently away from the team, so that he was forced to release his grip on the reins as he was hauled off his feet and jerked on to his back.

He vented a roar of alarm.

Edge said again to the growling dog, "Easy feller," as he backed across the alley with his burden.

The older man, with his attention divided between two areas of trouble, was making progress with the horse now that the German shepherd was moving away, staying close to Edge.

The half-breed halted his stooped-over back-tracking beside his own horse out front of the hotel and released his grip on John's collar.

By this time the young victim of the attack had recovered from alarm and was filled with a high anger as he fumbled to get a revolver out of his holster.

But instead of straightening to draw his own gun, Edge dropped to his haunches, left hand going into the long hair at the nape of his neck and coming out fisted around the handle of the straight razor. Which, in a blur or speed, was moved downward, so that the cool metal of the flat of the blade was resting across John's pulsing throat before the young man's gun was halfway out of the holster.

"Hey, mister! This horse is always spooked by dogs! John was just—"

John was about twenty-five. Tall and lean and strong, with a mean, unshaven face. Probably rode shotgun while the older man—who yelled the excuse—was the driver.

There was a stir of noise and activity. Some people hurrying toward the focal point of the excitement. Some eager to withdraw from it.

Once more the half-breed told the menacingly growling dog, "Easy, feller." Briefly glanced at the animal, who was standing on the other side of the terrified man with a sharply honed blade at his throat, then looked down at John again to say in the same tone of voice: "Push the gun back in, uh? And don't ever draw it against me in future unless it's to kill me."

"Edge, what the hell's happenin' here?" the

Lakeview sheriff demanded as he and a group of the other local citizens came to a halt in an arc across the street out front of The Webster House.

"I just told him to—" John started.

"My pa was a Mexican, feller," Edge cut in.

"What?" John rasped, flicking his eyes across their sockets to find the impassive face of the half-breed after they had sought out Sheriff Herman.

"I said my pa was a Mexican."

"What the hell, Edge?" Herman snarled and jerked aside his duster to drape a hand over the butt of his holstered Remington. "If you don't put away that blade and let John Cox get up on his feet—"

"Say Mexican, feller," Edge instructed.

The man swallowed hard and grimaced as this acted to push the skin of his thin throat harder against the blade of the razor. "What?"

"Say Mexican."

"Mexican, for Chri—"

"Fine, feller. So next time such an occasion arises, you'll say, 'Get that frigging dog out of sight, Mexican.' "

"Whatever you say."

"Edge, I'm warnin' you!" the sheriff snarled.

"I've said it," the half-breed told John Cox, and now he rose to his feet, bringing the razor up to the back of his neck and sliding it into the sheath.

Cox eased cautiously up into a sitting posture and the dog half circled around him to move in closer to the left heel of Edge.

The team horse, which had become calm now, began to toss his head and scrape at the ground with a forehoof as the dog changed position.

"Mister," the older member of the stage crew
said in a pleading tone, "I sure would appreciate
it if you'd get your dog off the street. This nag just
has a crazy hatred of any dog that gets this close
to him."

There was a mixture of lumbermen and mer-
chants in the group around Sheriff Herman. The
only woman close by was on the hotel stoop—a
fine-bodied, sour-faced woman in her forties in a
black dress and a white apron. She stood, her
arms folded across her ample bosom, directly in
front of the hotel's open doorway.

"Mrs. Webster?" Edge asked, tipping his hat to
her—as John Cox scrambled to his feet and hur-
ried across the alley mouth, scowling.

"Miss Webster!" the half-breed was corrected.

"You allow dogs in the hotel?"

"Never had had occasion to have a rule about
that before. But I guess me and my brother won't
have no objection to a dog. Long as he behaves
himself."

"You have a room available?"

"Certainly there's a room available. But what
applies to dogs, applies to people. They cause
any trouble, out they go."

A man emerged from the shaded lobby behind
her. A giant of a man close to seven feet tall and
perhaps weighing more than three hundred
pounds—little of his bulk comprised of excess fat.
Despite the fact that he had a naturally good-
humored face, in contrast with the soured look
that sculptured his sister's features, there was a
strong family resemblance between them. In the
light blueness of their eyes, the near whiteness of

their hair, and the cleft in their chins. He was in his early forties, she in her late.

"Any trouble, Max deals with it, Mr. Edge," Polly Webster said and cast a look of pride at her powerful brother. "He's good at that. But he'd just as soon take care of your horse or your luggage. Fix you up with a tub of hot water. Wash and press your clothes. That kind of service." She turned to go back into the hotel, and her brother, who was grinning foolishly, stepped out on to the stoop. The woman added, "You have only to ask."

"You bet, mister." Max confirmed.

The crowd began to disperse.

The stage driver snarled, "Don't be crazy, John!"

Edge whirled, instinctively reaching for the Frontier Colt in his holster as he adopted a half-crouched attitude, sideways on to the threat posed by the scowling young man intent upon revenge for his humiliation.

Cox was up on the high seat of the Concord and had been pretending to check that the roof baggage was secure while he listened to the exchange between Edge and Polly Webster—and came to a decision that he could not allow the matter to rest as it was. And so turned on the seat, a thumb cocking the hammer of the Winchester he had drawn from between two valises.

A chorus of gasps and rasped curses sounded from the stage passengers in process of boarding the Concord and the group that had begun to break up from around Herman.

Edge slid his revolver smoothly from the holster, thumbing back the hammer as he tilted the

Colt at his hip to aim the muzzle at the chest of the man with the rifle.

"Damnit!" the sheriff snarled, and squeezed the trigger of his Remington. Which had been clear of the holster and aimed before the stage driver shouted. For he had not turned away from the Concord, worried that the hotheaded youngster might not be able to hold his temper.

The bullet from the lawman's gun cracked toward John Cox a part of a second before a second revolver shot souded—this almost in perfect unison with the more deep throated report of the Winchester.

The young man on the Concord seat took the Remington bullet in his left shoulder and the impact of the lead into his flesh and against the bone half turned him, spoiling his aim with the rifle at the same instant the bullet from Edge's Colt drilled into the side of his head.

The rifle bullet went high and wide and probably cleared the two parallel streets of the town to splash harmlessly into the water far out in Mirror Lake.

By which time John Cox was slumped across the double seat of the stage, dead from the bullet that had blasted through his brain before coming to rest against the inside of his skull. A gush, then a trickle of crimson from the thick blackness of a sideburn marked the entry wound.

"Damnit to hell!" Sheriff Herman yelled to draw all but one pair of eyes to him after a tension-lengthened pause during which everyone stared at the corpse on the high seat. "I winged him, Edge! That was enough to stop him! You didn't have to kill him!"

The half-breed half cocked the Colt and turned the cylinder; thumbed aside the loading gate to extract the spent cartridge case. Then reloaded the revolver with a bullet from his belt. Only when the gun was back in the holster did he look at Herman to reply: "He was mad enough for a flesh wound not to stop him, sheriff. But that's beside the point, far as I'm concerned. Told him if he drew against me he'd have to kill me." Then he shifted his gaze, the slits of ice blue not glinting so brightly now the killing was done, to look at the massively built Max Webster. And asked, "Be much obliged if you'd have my horse taken care of, feller."

Max, with a confused frown, looked to his sister for guidance, and the sour-faced Polly urged, "Do as our new guest asks, Max."

"Hey, you gonna let this gunfighter get away with blastin' John into hell, Mr. Herman?" the driver asked bitterly.

"Clear case of self-defense," the lawman answered in a similar tone, and thrust the Remington back in its holster.

"But like you said, you winged him and John wouldn't've—"

"Get him down off of there and roll your rig outta here!" the sheriff cut in. "And let's everybody else attend to their own business!"

He glowered around at his fellow citizens and also included the passengers in the dictate with a dismissive gesture of his now empty gun hand.

Along both stretches of the street and at the intersections of the cross streets, a far larger audience had begun to form, drawn by the three gunshots.

Herman was the first to withdraw from the scene of violence, and began to snarl negative retorts to the queries that were voiced by those too late on the scene to see what had happened. Then, when the passengers got aboard the Concord and urged the driver to hurry to do what was ordered of him, the other local citizens moved off—most of them anxious to relate their version of events.

This as Max Webster came down off the hotel stoop and unhitched the horse while Edge and the dog stepped up and crossed the boarding to enter the lobby. Where, on the other side of the room crowded with overstuffed furniture and luxuriantly growing potted plants, Polly Webster stood behind a desk in an alcove. Flushed and breathing heavily, as if from a period of hard exertion—hard, but enjoyably exciting, since she seemed to be having difficulty in keeping a smile of satisfaction off her normally soured face.

"Room seven, which I can't say is the best in the house, Mr. Edge," she said breathlessly. "Because they are all equally good."

"It's the only one available, Miss Webster?" he asked as he zigzagged among the close-packed furnishings.

"We have no other guests at present, Mr. Edge. And please call me Polly. This is a very friendly hotel."

"That's nice, Miss Webster," he said as he

reached the front of the desk and she took a key off a row of eight numbered hooks. "That the room that's next to yours?"

She smiled. "It can get to be a very friendly hotel if. . ."

Her face was suddenly at its most sour as the start of a smile was wiped away, caused by Edge ignoring the proffered key to lean over the desk and take the one off the hook numbered 1.

"Figure this is the key to the room furtherest from yours, lady?"

"What's the matter with you, mister? Is a gun all you can shoot?"

He smiled and tipped his hat as he answered, "Keep thinking the worst of me and you could get lucky, Miss Webster."

"What the hell are you talking about?" she demanded.

"I get to make enemies easier than I make friends."

Chapter Nine

Edge, with the dog close on his heels, moved out of the lobby, along a dark hallway to the rear of the building, and up a flight of steps that angled toward the front. Followed numbered doors until he found that marked 1. The room was scrupulously clean, spartanly furnished, and very cold, with a small window that overlooked the alley between the hotel and the stage-line depot.

There was a single bed, a free-standing closet, a chair, a bureau, and a strip of carpet. Plain white walls with nothing hung on them and a whitened ceiling with a kerosene lamp suspended from its center. Beneath the blankets the linen was crisp and immaculately white. And in the top drawer of the bureau there was a Bible that looked as if it had never been opened. There was no dust, even inside the drawer.

The German shepherd sat close to the door whining his dislike of the confined space, and watched with sad eyes as Edge surveyed the contents of the room. His investigation completed, the half-breed turned the cane chair away from the window and sat facing the door. The dog moved across to sit beside him, thumping his tail on the floor a few times to register approval of the way his neck fur was being ruffled by one brown-skinned hand.

The left hand, which allowed the right to rest on the chair arm, ready to go inside the sheepskin coat and draw the Frontier Colt again should this be necessary.

After perhaps three minutes, footfalls sounded on the stairway and then the landing. The heavy footfalls of a man. They approached the door of Room 1 and halted. Knuckles rapped on the panel and Max Webster called:

"It's Max, Mr. Edge. Got your saddle and stuff. Okay to come in?"

Edge answered, "Sure thing," and although he showed no sign, tensed to reach for the holstered gun as he heard the latch rattle and then watched the door swing inwards.

The big man, with the half-breed's gear held easily under one arm, needed to duck his head to get through the doorway. And when he raised it again, it was to show that his face wore an expression of firm resolution. He dropped the gear on the floor and asked, as he closed the door, "Okay to dump it here, sir?"

The courtesy title did not match the look on his unintelligent face.

"Sure, Max. Just me being in here makes the place untidy, so why not—"

"Yeah, Polly's real house proud. Got this hatred for dirt. I'll be bringin' you up some water in a pitcher after, sir."

"After what, Max?"

In collecting so much brawn, it seemed that Max Webster had missed out on his full complement of brains. And Edge's comment and his response had sidetracked him from whatever he had felt needed to be said or done when he first entered the room.

"Oh, yeah, sir. Want you to know that you killin' that guy off the stage don't make me afraid of you."

The tension had begun to drain out of Edge, but now he got ready again to move his right hand to the butt of the revolver as he replied: "That was personal between Cox and me, feller. Wasn't meant to be—"

"So don't you try no funny business with my sister, sir. Or I'll make you regret the day you ever came to Lakeview." He wrapped the palm of his right hand over the fist of his left and made the knuckles crack one at a time.

"What if she sets her cap at me, Max?"

"You tell her no, sir. And you either go see Rita down at the Treasure House or you take a swim in Mirror Lake. You know what I mean, sir?"

"Sure thing, Max."

"That's good, sir. I'll go bring the water now. Leave it outside the door for you to get when you're ready. In case you don't wanna be disturbed. You have a nice stay with us, you hear?"

Edge nodded.

The big man opened the door and ducked his head to step out of the room. Then paused to look back, a sheepish expression on his face, as he said: "Ain't got nothin' against you, sir. Tell it to every stranger that comes to Lakeview. Same as I've warned off every man that lives around here. Man crazy she is, and I ain't gonna let her get to be like that Rita Cornell down at the saloon."

Edge nodded again and Max went off the threshold, closed the door, and moved away down the landing and then the stairs. After which, the only sounds to be heard were muffled by distance into a low, murmuring hum comprised of all kinds of noises made by the citizens of Lakeview engaging their early-afternoon activities.

After listening to the background sound for a few moments, the half-breed moved from the chair to the bed and stretched out on his back. He heard Max approach and then withdraw as he delivered the promised pitcher of water.

The dog padded across to the door and curled up in front of it, ears pricked for any suspicious sounds while his eyes gazed unblinkingly at the man on the bed. Edge had now tipped his hat forward to cover his face, not to encourage sleep, for he needed none after his better than eight hours of rest in the cabin across the lake. Instead, as an aid to concentration while he reflected on the recent past and endeavored to find some logic in the way he had responded to outside influences.

Barny Galton had willed him the claim, and his time spent working it and sharing the isolated existence with the big German shepherd had been fine. Perhaps there had not been a better time since his tragically short marriage to Beth when they worked the Dakotas farm together.

He grunted into the semidarkness under the

Stetson, not wanting to delve that far back into the past. The dog raised his head and cocked it, as if expecting the sound to be followed by a command. But no word was spoken and the animal misinterpreted the grunt for a snore, rose, and padded back to the bed. Where he sat down and rested his head on the bedcovers.

This as the half-breed's face, heavily bristled with a half day's growth of beard, grimaced under the hat, the expression triggered by the recollection of how he had allowed Ralph and Janet Galton to take over the claim unscathed, despite the aggressiveness of their approach to him.

The lines of the grimace, hidden to the intelligent eyes of the dog, deepened into the heritage and element-browned skin of the lean face. This as his mind conjured up a series of vivid images so that he relived his fatal run-in with the young John Cox. Who might not have died had the day started better for Edge.

The German shepherd put a paw on the bed and laid his ears back, expecting to be ordered down. But the man made no sound outside of his regular intake and exhalation of breath. So the dog came half off his haunches, extended the other front paw, and slithered rather than jumped on the the bed. To lay alongside Edge, still disconsolately expectant of a harsh-voiced order for several seconds. Then sighed with relief certain the man was asleep and unaware that he had canine company on the bed.

Edge had no regret about taking another life. The kid off the stage had insulted the Mexican side of the half-breed and been paid out for that with a bad scare. And he had been warned about drawing his gun. One of the few rules that Edge lived by insisted that Cox die for ignoring that warning. All that was questionable was the degree of the scare and its parallel humiliation, which had caused the kid to go for the Winchester.

Should a portion of the enmity he had unleashed against John Cox have been in truth directed at the Galtons?

And a little should surely have been aimed at the Lakeview lawman for his arrogance in ordering Edge to remain in town until—the way it turned out—another stranger gave or did not give the all clear for him to leave.

Then, probably the largest share of all the ice-cold anger he had felt when he dragged the kid to the ground and put the razor to his throat should have been turned inwards. Because of the way he had compliantly agreed to go along with a course of events that under normal circumstances would have gone against his grain. In short, he had allowed others to dictate what he should do. And that was not his way at all, unless the pattern of the future mapped out by others matched that which he would have elected to follow himself.

The dog sighed again, long and louder than before, causing his whole body to quiver. And immediately became alert when the man spoke from beneath the hat.

"Yeah, I know how you feel, feller. This ain't our style at all. And I figure we ought to do something about it before we start in to sit up and beg whenever anybody snaps their fingers."

He lifted the hat off his face and the dog ran a wet tongue across a stubbled cheek as he thudded his leg with his tail.

"Glad you agree, feller."

Edge swung his feet to the floor on one side of the bed and the dog jumped heavily off the other side.

In the distance to the west of town, the steam whistle at the sawmill shrilled a signal that it was time for the afternoon's work to start.

Edge said. "Hell, feller, I forgot that to get some feed for you was the reason we headed for this town in the first place."

The dog whined and went to the door as the half-breed stood up from the bed. Then, while the man gathered up his saddle and bedroll, the animal sat down but constantly shuffled back and forth on his rump, obviously impatient to be outside and heading for his next meal. Though when Edge opened the door, the dog contained himself and held back, waiting to fall in at his left heel. Then the animal, previously too preoccupied with the excitement of leaving, heard a sound that erupted a growl from deep in his throat.

The half-breed froze just as he was about to step out on to the landing, the smile for the German shepherd displaced by a thin-lipped coldness as he made to drop his burdens and reach for the holstered Colt.

But then Polly Webster swept into view outside the open door, a towel in one hand and the pitcher of water delivered earlier by her brother in the other. On her flushed face a lopsided grin which the smell of her breath stressed was caused largely by liquor.

"Don't look so scared, Mr. High-and-Mighty Edge," she slurred, leaning a shoulder against the doorjamb as she swayed and almost fell. "I ain't come to rape you. Just brought you up the towel my dumb-assed brother forgot. Seems he forgot how to come through a door, too. Dumb cluck left the water out here on the—"

She started to come into the room, but Edge was already moving to leave, holding the saddle in front of him so that she bumped into this before being forced to back up.

"Obliged to you for taking the trouble, lady," he told her and glimpsed the latent fury in her crystal-clear, light blue eyes before she wrenched them away from the trap of his slitted, ice blue gaze. "But me and this feller have decided to check out. Willing to pay for a day's rent of the room. No need of any other services."

His eyes flicked across their sockets to survey the landing in both directions and the securely closed doors to either side—the head of the stairs at the end. Certain of only one thing about this new situation: that whether she had taken one or a dozen shots of rye whisky to taint her breath, Polly Webster was only feigning being drunk. Which had to mean she was trying to stir up trouble of some kind for him. And surely this would involve her giant brother.

"You don't bad mouth me and get away with it, you bastard!" she rasped softly as he turned in front of her to move toward the stairway, the tense but no longer growling German shepherd as close as ever behind him. And then she raised her voice to a shrill pitch to shriek: "Max! Help me, Max! He hurt me! God in Heaven, he made me. . ."

She let the lie hang unfinished in the chill, silent atmosphere of the hotel landing. Then ended the silence with the first of a series of explosive sobs. The second of which sounded in unison with the smashing of the water pitcher on the polished floor of the landing. The third closely followed by the crash of broken glass.

He had his head turned to look back at her by then. In time to see her bring an almost full bottle of whisky out from under the towel and smash it against the doorframe—letting go of the neck as the glass and timber made contact. Next, starting to bring the towel up to her face, to hide her unbloodshot and tearless eyes in its fabric.

Briefly, her spite-filled eyes locked with the hooded gaze of the man she suddenly realized she had misjudged. Her all-consuming malice was abruptly swept away, to leave her in the grip of terror. So that there was genuine emotion to power the body-wrenched sob that sounded as she buried her now pale face in the towel. A sob which also had an accompanying sound—that of a door jerked angrily open at the foot of the stairs.

"I'm sorry!" she wailed through the muffle of the towel. "You mustn't hurt Max! He's only—"

"Hold on, sis!" her brother bellowed as his footfalls thudded heavily on the stairway. "I'm comin'! You better lay off Polly, you filthy sonofabitch!"

Edge dropped his bedroll and saddle and took a step toward the almost hysterical woman. Brought his trailing leg forward and up to thud the knee into the base of her belly.

With a cry of pain she dropped the towel and reached with both hands to the source of the agony, folding double in an attempt to ease the fire started by the blow. She screamed again as the half-breed's other knee slammed into her face. The impact forced her to straighten, then flung her out on to her back, her arms going wide to the sides and her legs splaying in a vain attempt to retain her balance.

This just as her massively built brother half fell up the final few steps of the stairs and shuddered to a halt at the far end of the landing, his towering, broad frame blocking out much of the light from the window in back of him. But he had seen his sister spread-eagled on the floor some fifty feet away, as she brought both her arms in from the sides to claw at the base of her belly; not yet conscious of the blood that the blow to her face had spurted from her nostrils.

Max stared with limitless loathing at the shorter, leaner man who stood beside the terrified and agonized woman. A man who spoke a couple of gentle words to quiet his dog, massaged his knees by turns, and slowly slid the Winchester from the scabbard attached to his discarded saddle.

An expression of total indifference on his face, Edge drawled, "How the lady looks, don't guess there's any way I can convince you I didn't lay a hand on her, Max?"

Chapter Ten

Polly Webster began to tremble and wail as her brother did his knuckle-cracking trick and started along the landing in a slow, shuffling gait.

Edge brought up the rifle to aim it at the big man from his hip and the German shepherd whined softly—confused because he sensed a dangerous situation and had been ordered to stay out of it.

"I'll kill you, Max." the half-breed warned evenly.

"You don't scare me, mister. I told you that, already."

"A man that's as big as you and as mad as you sure scares me, feller. Killing you is the only way I know to stop you."

"You don't scare me."

"I'm impressed. But you shouldn't get yourself killed for a lie."

Polly curtailed her crying to demand in a croaking voice: "Stop this, Max! He's right!"

The big man kept on coming. "I warned him off

you, sis. And if he's gonna kill me, he's gonna kill me. Let one filthy bastard get away with it and before you know it there won't be no difference between that Rita Cornell and you."

"But he didn't do nothing to me, Max!" she implored. "I was only pretending!"

The massively built man halted about fifteen feet along the landing from where Edge stood with the leveled Winchester. The half-breed, between his saddle and bedroll, watched Max impassively, while the dog, just behind him, looked eagerly from brother to sister and back.

Edge, not daring to move his gaze away from the big man, heard without seeing as the woman struggled painfully into a half-slumped sitting posture, one shoulder against the wall. And reached for the towel to stanch the trickle of blood from her nostrils.

"What you mean, sis?" Max asked, coming down off the peak of aggression as his suspicious eyes shifted away from the half-breed's face for the first time in many stretched seconds. To look down and to the side at his sister. "You look to me like you got hurt real bad."

He cracked his knuckles, no longer wanting desperately to free his fist from the other hand and smash it into the unblinking face of Edge.

Polly Webster began to weep, but tears of misery instead of pain now.

Edge pursed his lips and let out some pent-up breath. Then muttered, "Me and the dog are hungry, lady."

The weeping stopped and the woman began to

speak, very fast. While the anger renewed its hold on Max, but was no longer directed at the half-breed.

"He turned me down when he first checked in, Max. I offered myself to him and he turned me down and insulted me. So I planned to get back at him. Waited for you to take your nap and came up here to his room. Pretended to be drunk. Was going to tell you he got me that way and —and—and then took advantage of me. Wanted you to come up here and beat the daylights out of him. To get back at him. For the way he turned me down flat when I all but threw myself at him." She paused to draw breath and a sob burst from her.

Max groaned bitterly, "Not again, sis?"

"But right at the last I knew I'd made a mistake, Max. A bad one. I knew at the start he was a mean one. The way he killed the stage guard. But I never thought he'd kill you and me—"

"Mistakes happen, lady," Edge cut in on the now virtually babbling woman. "Me and the dog are getting hungrier, Max. Do I need to kill you to get out of this place?"

The big man withdrew his fist from the clutch of the opposite palm and dropped his arms to his sides. Shrugged his broad shoulders and looked like he was set to cry. And threatened by such an emotion, his unintelligent face took on the quality of a child's.

"What can I tell you, sir?" he pleaded.

"I know as much as I need to, feller. Figure I could guess the rest if I wanted to take the time and trouble."

"Wish you hadn't hit her."

"It was hurt her or kill her, feller. Way I was getting close to drowning in the shit I been taking lately."

The woman with blood on her face was weeping very softly now. But was not wallowing too deeply in the well of self-pity for all else to be excluded from her sensibilities. She was immediately silent when Sheriff Herman called from down in the hotel lobby:

"Anybody home?"

The dog barked once and Edge eased the Winchester's hammer forward and began to slide the rifle back in the scabbard. Then glanced at the woman as he lifted his saddle and bedroll up from the floor.

The lawman could be heard moving along the hallway to the foot of the stairs, where he halted. "No trouble, boy. Just want a word with your master."

Edge saw the bitter disappointment on Polly Webster's face and knew she had been ready to switch her story again if the opportunity arose. A scorned woman willing to go to almost any length to vent her spite against the man who spurned her. Knowing she could control the moods of her dullard brother but resigned to defeat now that the Lakeview lawman was a witness.

The half-breed called: "Stay there, sheriff. I'm on my way down."

"Just came to tell you that you can leave town any time you like, Edge," Herman answered.

"Town and the hotel?" the half-breed asked of Max, who was blocking the way to the head of the stairs for a man with a bulky burden under each arm. "After I pay for the room. The breakages are all down to you sister, feller."

Max folded flat to a closed door in a recess to allow Edge by. And growled: "No charge sir. Least I can do, I reckon. Appreciate it if you didn't put it around?"

Edge drew back his lips to display a brief smile as he replied: "I don't. And that's what caused the trouble." Then shifting his glinting-eyed gaze from the saddened Max to the now glowering Polly, added, "So I can't say I'm obliged to you for having me, lady!"

"Two words for you, mister!" she rasped venomously. "And the second one's off!"

"Aw, sis," Max groaned.

This as Edge reached the top of the stairway and looked down at the grim-faced Lakeview lawman, who stood at the foot, shoulders hunched and hands thrust deep in the pockets of his duster.

Herman started his explanation as soon as the half-breed, the eager dog at his heels, began to descend.

"Lee Galton just got back to town, Edge. In bad shape. Seems his brother and sister-in-law jumped him out at the claim. Beat up on him and kicked him off. Family dispute which ain't none of my business unless they start in to kill one another. But far as you're concerned, Lee Galton did find out the others dug up old Barny's body. And saw he died like you said. Of the gangrene from havin' his leg torn off."

Edge had reached the foot of the stairs by now.

And in the otherwise quietness of the hotel, an exchange of angry whispering between the Webster brother and sister could be heard, but not understood.

"Obliged."

The lawman's suspicious gaze shifted from the half-breed to the head of the stairs and back again. "Looked like you were fixin' to leave this hotel anyway?"

"And it doesn't matter now if I was going to ride out of the town as well, sheriff."

A shrug of the shoulders. "That's right."

Herman stood aside for Edge to lead the way along the gloomy hall and across the lobby. Fell in behind the German shepherd and then lengthened his stride to get ahead at the closed door. Where he halted, a hand on the latch. "I ain't the smartest man in the world, mister. But I ain't the most stupid either. Me gettin' here when I did broke up trouble between you and the Websters."

"It did, sheriff."

"Don't surprise me. Been some time since Polly set her cap at anybody and Max went crazy at the poor slob for tryin' to take a bite of the apple shoved under his nose. Glad I stopped it goin' too far this time. But don't you take it no further, Edge. In case you ain't so lucky to have so many eye witnesses to self-defense the next time. Afternoon to you."

He lifted the latch, jerked open the door, and swung out. Stepped down from the stoop and angled across the street toward his office. With a swagger in his gait, like he was proud of having issued the warning.

The German shepherd gave a short, sharp bark and the half-breed murmured:

"Sure, feller. Let's go fill our bellies and get the hell out to where you're the only one gives me orders."

The afternoon air was colder than the morning's had been and there was a bank of white cloud streaked with gray in the east. But it had a long way to spread to threaten the bright sun that was far advanced on its down slide toward the southwestern horizon. But maybe by nightfall the weather would close in on this section of the Montana Rockies. Perhaps to herald an early winter that would maintain a tight grip on the timber-clad slopes and high rock ridges all the way through to next spring.

The prospect of this happening occupied Edge as he and the dog moved along the street toward a building with a sign that read *Good Food —Epicure Restaurant—Fine Wines.* And caused him to quicken his pace as he contemplated being snowed up in Lakeview for months at a time. Which was an image not difficult to retain on this deserted street in this quiet town under a bright but vaguely menacing sky.

Then, as he neared the restaurant, the town was not quite so quiet, for he heard hoofbeats closing in from the east. Then, when he stepped up on to the sidewalk and dumped his gear against the wall to the side of the restaurant's glass-panel door, he saw a trio of men slow their mounts from a canter to a walk as they came off the spur of the trail to advance along the street.

Hard-looking men in thick, dark-colored topcoats that made it difficult to judge how they were built, all wearing gloves and with the collars of their coats turned up and their hats pulled down. Red-rimmed eyes and unshaven jaws. Element-stained flesh pinched blue by a long time riding through the cold day. All in their mid-thirties and in a bad humor.

The one who rode in the center, the meanest-looking of the three, a sneer in his tone to match the one on his face, growled, "Place a man can get a warmin' drink of liquor in this dump of a town?"

The newcomers were still several yards short of where Edge had pushed open the door of the restaurant after telling the dog to sit by his gear, so the spokesman had to shout the query.

The half-breed waited until the men were level with him, so he could reply without raising his voice: "Keep on along the street. Place called the Treasure House couple of blocks down on the right."

They went on by without a word or sign of acknowledgment and Edge stepped into the restaurant. The skin of his hands and face immediately starting to tingle in the stove heat of the small room with its half dozen cloth-covered, chair-ringed tables and lone occupant. Who said wearily:

"Guess you'll want the biggest steak I have. Cooked until it's burnt black and served with an enormous portion of—"

"No, feller," the half-breed cut in on the fifty-year-old, five-foot-tall, and very fat man, bringing a flashing smile to his round, many, chinned face with its bulging cheeks and thin black moustache. Which quickly evaporated when his sole customer went on: "Like six steaks cooked that way. One on a plate with a heap of whatever's available. The others cut up and in a bowl for my dog."

He took off his hat and coat and hung them on one of the row of pegs to the side of the door. And sat at the nearest table. "Some hot soup while I'm waiting for the meat would be good, feller. And I'd be obliged if you'd hurry it up. Looks like it could snow before long and I want—"

The restauranteur, who was dressed in a faded and frayed dinner jacket, white shirt, and black bow tie, had not moved from the archway beside the stove across from the door. And seemed speechless until he blurted,

"The best chef outside of San Francisco does not cook the best meat in the Territory of Montana for a dog!"

Edge took out the makings and began to roll a cigarette. Said evenly as he tipped tobacco into the strip of paper: "No sweat, feller. My dog ain't that fussy. Heard from his previous owner that he'll eat raw meat that's a little old. Special kind of meat, that is."

"All right, all right, I'll go fix your order, mister!" the man said, suddenly wan faced as he whirled to go through the archway into the kitchen out back. From where he called; "Only I don't have no soup that can be ready before the steaks!"

"No sweat," Edge answered as he licked the paper.

"Patience is one of the virtues I do have." He struck a match on his holstered Colt to light the cigarette and added, "Guess the fine wines aren't chilled, either?"

"Not the white ones, no," the man in the kitchen admitted sourly as frying fat began to sizzle. "I got some first-class reds at room temperature, but I don't guess—"

"That's right," Edge put in. And just for a moment had a vivid recollection of the house at Stormville where Adam Steele had been indulging in what he considered the good things of life—including fine wines—before he, Edge, came to dinner and brought that interlude to an end. And he kept the quiet smile in place as he went on: "Only as a last resort if there's no beer or whisky, feller. Like most people around Lakeview, I figure?"

"It's an old sign," the man confirmed, needing to speak louder as he put meat in the skillet and the sizzling sound rose in volume. "Set up here after the gold grubbers left and the lumber men moved in. Figured to attract the carriage trade, but it never did work out. Them that make the biggest piles go home to their lakefront mansions to eat and them that do the work ain't got nothin' left to spend on decent eatin' after they handed over to their women and drunk away most of the rest down at Leo Evers's place. And them that ain't got women and brats, they spend big at the Treasure House, most of them. And even them that don't, all they want is what you're havin'. Epicure Restaurant, that's rich. Wasn't for a handful of people of taste that come in every now and then, I'd

change the name to something like The Feedin'
Trough."

"Lakeview started out as a mining town, feller?" Edge asked as he leaned back comfortably
in the chair, enjoying the cigarette and relishing
the warmth of the small restaurant.

"Wasn't big enough be called a town in those
days, mister," the man in the kitchen replied eagerly, obviously pleased to have somebody to
talk to. "Just the one general store in a regular
buildin' and a few other enterprises in tents.
Right on the lakeshore. Claims out in every direction and not one of them a rich one.

"Then a group of prospectors saw there was a
better livin' to be made out of the timber that just
had to be cut down—not grubbed out of the
ground. And Lakeview ain't never looked back
since. Me included, mister, far as makin' some
bucks is concerned. Just riles me sometimes that
the skills I learned in some of the best carriage-
trade hotels in San Francisco ain't hardly ever
called on to be used in this town."

There was a tall window on either side of the
restaurant door, with net curtains hung from
rails halfway down them: but more effectively
screened by the mist of condensation. And this
blocking off of any view of the street acted to in-
tensify the sense of being detached from a troubled and cold world—allowed a respite in safe surroundings filled with pleasant sensations.

"Still, I guess I didn't ought to complain. Done
better than a lot of folks that set up business here
. . ."

The man in the kitchen went on talking about

Lakeview's history and some of the more unfortunate who had peopled it. Voice raised to be heard above the sizzling of the frying steaks, the aroma of which mingled with and then masked the smell of burning tobacco.

Edge listened with mild interest, and did not fail to remain attentive, even during the period when the German shepherd distracted him. First as a condensation-blurred face at a window, the dog up on his hind legs, forepaws on the ledge, trying to see into the restaurant, head cocking to one side and then the other. Perhaps whining softly in distress that Edge was not in sight. But no sound from the animal heard because of the low and constant moaning of a wind that had sprung up moments earlier. For several minutes the half-breed tried to ignore the dog, who sometimes had to drop down from the window to rest his hind legs. But then he gave in to the animal with a soft curse.

Got up from the table and went to the door, which he cracked open to arc the butt of his cigarette on to the street. Saw the wind, which was from the east, snatch at it and drive it hard along the street. Then looked down and saw the dog sitting in front of the door, fur ruffled by the wind and eyes pleading to be allowed entrance, a soft whine adding to the entreaty.

Edge just mouthed a curse now, then put a forefinger to his lips and opened the door a little more. The man in the kitchen was saying:

". . . was another man figured the lumber men would spend their money on inconsequentials and found out the hard way they . . ." Then either heard the louder sounds or the weather when the door was opened or felt the draft of cold air reaching across the dining room and through the archway on the far side. And he called anxiously: "You're not leavin'? Won't be but a few minutes now!"

He showed his worried face at the arch, obviously leaning back from the stove, where his hands remained busy. Then he smiled his relief as he saw Edge seated again at the table.

"Just got rid of my cigarette, feller," the half-breed said, pressing hard with his right hand on the neck of the German shepherd to force him down on to his belly. Which the dog was reluctant to do while his nostrils twitched to the delicious aroma of frying meat. Then, to have something to say, Edge asked, "The Websters been in town since it got started as a lumber center, feller?"

The man went from sight at the archway, the query taking his mind off the odd, sideways-leaning position of Edge. Who now glowered down at the dog in an eyeball-to-eyeball confrontation that caused the animal to whimper and lower himself to his belly, ears back and eyes requesting forgiveness.

The ice went from the glinting blue slits of the man's eyes and he stroked the dog's head.

"Polly and Max, mister?" the man in the kitchen said eagerly. "They're a strange pair, aren't they? Neither of them quite normal. Max, as you no doubt judged for yourself, is a little short up top? Hopefully, you will not have been long enough at the hotel to have discovered just what it is makes his sister . . ."

He was from Ireland, and the accent of the land of his birth became more pronounced in his voice as he warmed to his subject. Which was totally immaterial. But then so was the information the man was imparting about the Webster brother and sister. So why had he asked about them?

Because he had needed to cover his smuggling of the dog into the restaurant. He could just as well have asked about the wind and if it was the kind that brought rain or snow to this part of the country.

Shit, what did it matter about the weather? It didn't. Just as it didn't matter where the man came from. Or what he thought of the Websters.

But why should he feel it necessary to smuggle the dog in out of the cold. Dammit, it was yet another example of him doing something in a way that was not his style at all.

The man with the strong Irish accent was explaining how Polly Webster had been engaged to be married to the son of a rich lumberman many years earlier. But he was killed by a falling tree and Polly was driven almost crazy with grief. Which she then overcame by going with any man who would take her. There were a great many who went with her before her brother discovered what was happening. Max possessed a sense of morality that was as strong as his body and he made it known in Lakeview that he would break every bone in the body of any man who went with his sister outside of wedlock.

"And never was a Lakeview man who took the risk of gettin' that badly beaten up," the man said as he came out from the archway, a plate in one hand and a bowl in the other, both heaped with steaming food. "And none wanted to get hitched to such a sour-tempered woman, that's for sure."

The dog could contain himself no longer as the mouth-watering aroma of cooked meat got stronger by the moment. He leaped to his feet and vented a sharp bark of impatience, would maybe have sprung toward the suddenly angry and frightened restaurateur had Edge not hooked a restraining hand under the rope collar.

"This is too much!" the man snapped, his accent now back to the false camp American that he had used when Edge first came into his restaurant. He banged the plate and the bowl down on the nearest table and folded his arms across his fleshy chest, the gesture one of determination while his multi-chinned face expressed a look that indicated he was ready to turn and run if the hungry dog was released. "I agree to cook first-class meat for your animal, mister! As a special favor to you. But I refuse to serve the food to the dog in my dinin' room. And unless you get the creature out of here, I will refuse to serve you. I allow men to bring dogs in here, the next thing you know, they'll be bringin' in their horses!"

"Easy, feller," Edge said to the dog and let go of the collar as he rose from the chair. Mentally breathed a sigh of relief when the animal did not launch into a spring at the table where the steaming food had been set down. Instead, he remained close at heel as the half-breed went toward the table and the man, arms still folded but chins trembling, backed off. "We all need standards or I guess we get to be worse than animals, feller," the tall man said evenly to the shorter one as he sat down at the new table and carefully removed the bowl of meat from its cloth-covered top to the floor—and nodded to the dog that he could eat. "And I go along with the one you have about not allowing animals in your restaurant."

"So why are you—" the man started as Edge pulled his plate in front of him and picked up the ready-laid knife and fork.

"But you've caught me on a strange kind of day, feller. I even keep surprising myself, so I guess there's no way anyone else can understand."

The dog was halfway through wolfing down the bowl of best steak. But interrupted his ravenous feeding to briefly raise his head and rest it against the half-breed's thigh.

Edge told the dog: "I bought you lunch, feller. So eat it. We'll talk about this whole crazy business later."

The dog returned his attention to the bowl of food.

The restaurateur backed all the way to the side of the arch, where he shook his head and eyed his customer with a brand of nervous disdain as he accused, "Crazy is right, mister!"

Edge had started to eat the meal now and showed no sign of being mad at the man for the taunt. Which bolstered his courage so that he felt able to growl with heavy sarcasm:

"Always thought it was your horse your kind was supposed to fall in love with!"

The half-breed glanced down at the German shepherd, who had finished the meat and was

now seated on his haunches, looking up as he
licked his lips in appreciation of the food while
his eyes showed gratitude for it.

"No sweat, feller," Edge said to the dog and
grinned as he added: "It's something like the old
story. My horse don't understand me."

Chapter Eleven

The dog lay in quiet contentment under the table while the half-breed finished the meal. And the man beside the archway was sullenly silent until pride in his trade as a chef got the better of his prejudice.

And he murmured, "I have to admit your dog is better behaved than some of the two-legged customers I get in here, mister."

Edge simply nodded in acknowledgment, while he chewed a mouthful of the tenderest and tastiest steak he had eaten for a very long time.

"And it's a real pleasure for me to see somebody eatin' with so much enjoyment—not just to fill an emptiness in their stomach, if you know what I mean?"

Edge nodded again, swallowed some more meat, and answered: "There's food and food, feller. And hunger and hunger. You're a real fine cook and I had the right kind of appetite to appreciate this food."

Which opened the way for the man by the arch to start in to talk once more. He looked enthusias-

tically ready to begin when hooves were heard
clopping on the street again. The horses were
being ridden from the western side of town, and
were held to a walk. The man came away from the
rear wall to go toward the front of his restaurant.

"Maybe the strangers you talked to earlier,
mister. Needin' something good and solid to soak
up the rotgut Leo Evers has been sellin' them."

He had to pass close by the table where Edge
sat and came to a halt as he did so, worried by a
growl from the dog underneath.

"Friend, feller," the half-breed said soothingly.

And the man blew some cool air up over his
face as he continued on to the door. Opened it an
inch or so, but then fought to close it again, needing to use force to beat the power of the height-
ened wind that sought to tear it from his grasp.
This as the brightness faded from the daylight,
the cloud bank having spread fast to blanket the
sky and mask the sinking sun of late afternoon.

The restauranteur used a sleeve of his black
dinner jacket to clear a patch of condensation
from the glass panel of the door. And pressed his
face close to the panel as Sheriff Herman's voice
was raised to sound above the moan of the wind
between buildings and the slow clop of many
hooves on the street.

"Just you listen to what I got to say, you people!"

The riders kept their horses coming along the
street in the same steady cadence as before. Until
a pistol shot sounded from the midtown area, and
then the mounts were reined in, directly outside

the restaurant as the man with his face to the cleared space on the window gasped:

"Oh, my goodness."

The German shepherd growled his dislike of the atmosphere and its sound effects and Edge calmed him.

The Lakeview lawman did not close with the stalled riders, so had to continue to shout above the wind noise.

"One Galton brother beatin' up on another is family trouble and none of mine. But if I get any kinda complaint about folks not in that family causin' a ruckus that's against the law, I'll take steps!"

There was a pause of stretched seconds, as if the listeners were waiting for the speaker to complete something left unfinished. Until a man among the listeners yelled, "That all, sheriff?"

A briefer pause, then Herman countered with an angry tone: "Yeah, except to tell you I think you're all outta your minds! I got more chance of makin' president of the United States than anybody has of strikin' it rich on Barny Galton's claim!"

The man at the door growled, "Ain't that a fact, Eddie Herman," and turned away from his vantage point.

This just as the wind veered again and gusted, to wrench open the door, which he had not securely latched a few moments ago. The sound of the door crashing against the inside wall and the blast of icy air dispelling the stove heat of the restaurant caused Edge to look across the room just as he rattled his fork down on the empty plate.

And he was in time to see a line-abreast-group of six men start their horses forward.

One was the yellow-bearded, dark-eyed Lee Galton, who now had a puffed and discolored right cheek and a white dressing above his left eye. Another was the pipe-smoking old man who had been outside a house on a cross street when Edge first rode into town. A third was the kid with the sack who had spoken to him shortly afterwards. There was another old-timer and a second teenage kid. And there was Max Webster.

All of them, hunched deep into the protection of warm coats and with the chin straps of their hats cinched tight, looked at the front of the restaurant when the door crashed open. But only the big man with the brain of a dullard did a double take at Edge seated at the table, and directed a warning look at the halfbreed that he emphasized by folding a fist in the palm of the other hand. And perhaps cracked his knuckles. But the wind would have masked the sound. A second later the door had been fought closed. Then the riders demanded a faster pace from their mounts and in a very short time all sounds of the group's departure were lost under the moan of the wind.

"Get rich quick," the restauranteur mumbled as he returned to his accustomed place beside the arch—making sure he circled wide of the table with the over protective dog lurking quietly beneath. "You see them out there, mister? The young, the old, and the stupid? Led by a stranger who does not know any better. Ever since the first of them lakefront mansions was built, everybody's wanted to have one."

He shook his head sadly and shrugged his shoulders. "Even me, one time. Figured to make a pile out of this place and build me a fine house down there on the lake. But I soon gave up that ambition and settled for the best I could get. Like most of us did.

"That Polly Webster, though, she ain't never given up dreamin'. Maybe because she almost made it—would have been livin' in a mansion by the lake now if her beau hadn't been crushed by that tree. So it was her put Max up to ridin' out with that Galton, I'm bettin'. When even he has the sense to know there ain't no pay dirt worth the diggin'—"

"How much I owe for the food, feller?" Edge cut in as he pushed back his chair and stood up, lighting the cigarette he had rolled while the man gave his unasked-for opinions of the six-man expedition to the claim across the lake.

The German shepherd was out from under the table and standing beside the half-breed's left leg almost before the man was fully erect.

"Two dollars," came the reply, with a disappointed expression, like the man was sorry to lose his lone customer and audience.

"Worth double, feller." Edge said and brought out his bankroll to peel off the m money.

"Only want what I ask for mister."

"All you're getting," Edge told him, dropped the two bills beside his empty plate, and went toward the place where his hat and coat hung beside the door. "Giving an opinion is all."

He had them both on, the coat buttoned, and was fixing the chin strap of the hat when shadowy

forms moved on the other side of the nearest
misted window, booted feet rang on the hollow
sidewalk, and the door was pushed open. And a
man rasped an obscenity when the gusting wind
wrenched the door from his hand.

There were three of them—the men who had
ridden into Lakeview earlier and asked Edge
where they could get a drink. They did not look as
if they had enjoyed themselves at the Treasure
House, nor warmed themselves. But they smelled
like they had swallowed a lot of liquor trying.
Then, with the door firmly closed at their backs,
to block off the blast of cold and fresh air, they
smelled of staler odors.

They were as hard eyed and rugged faced as
they had seemed from a distance. The top man
close to forty and the other two a year or so over
thirty. All around six feet in height with lean and
powerful builds that their thick topcoats did not
conceal. With unkempt black hair and crooked
teeth a long way from white. Unshaven and
maybe unwashed for many days. The kind of men
it was difficult to visualize as children. Whose
life-styles invariably meant they never got to be
elderly. And who appeared to be scowling even
when they smiled.

Like now, as the top man breathed in deeply
through his nose and said, as the other two imitated him: "Ain't that beautiful, boys? Part of
everyone's dream of home—the smell from the
kitchen while mom's cookin' supper."

"If you fellers have got the appetites, I have the
food to satisfy them," the little man with the many
chins said eagerly, flashing a bright smile as he

gestured with a hand to encompass all the unoccupied tables. "Sit anyplace you like, gentlemen, And tell me what I can get you."

"Three of the biggest steaks you got, mister," the top man answered with a smack of his thin lips. "Fried black. And with no dog hairs on the side, uh?"

He moved away from the door and the two younger men followed him. The one who had a constant tic just below his right eye growled:

"That's right, Lester. And I guess we better be careful where we step, in case there'a any dog crap in here."

The man with eyes that were cracked as narrow as those of Edge, but were a glistening green in color, added, "I think I can smell dog pee, Lester."

The restauranteur licked his smiling lips nervously and went to the table closest to the arch that gave access to the kitchen. And spoke quickly as he half circled it, pulling out three chairs. "Here, gentlemen. Sit here. The dog was not in this area at all. And I did tell him dogs are not allowed in my establishment. But he refused to remove him and there was nothin' I could do about it. But I can assure you the animal did not perform any natural functions in here and came nowhere near my kitch . . ."

Lester and his partners moved to the proffered chairs and sat down while the excitable fat man was giving the fast-spoken assurances. On the way unbuttoned their coats to display the gunbelts slung around their narrow waists. And it was the final jerking to the side of their coats to reveal

the holstered revolvers that caused the owner of
the place to abandon what he was saying and
back off from the table, gulping hard. Then licking his lips again, with a quicker movement of his
tongue, he looked across the dining room and
found his eyes firmly held in the trap of the half-
breed's coldly glinting gaze. But next expressed
relief with a smile and a sigh when Edge gave a
curt nod and shifted his attention to the trio of
newcomers slumped arrogantly in their chairs at
the table; weary, chilled, hungry, liquored-up,
and looking for trouble.

The man with green eyes instructed, "Go start
cookin' up the chow, fatso."

This as Edge moved to the door, the German
shepherd right on his heels, and reached for the
latch.

"That dog a fighter, mister?" Lester asked.

The half-breed answered, "He sure ain't no
boxer, feller."

The fat man directed a strange look at Edge
from the doorway. An expression of entreaty that
perhaps begged him to leave fast before trouble
started, or maybe pleaded for him to stay to deal
with it.

The man with the constant tic vented a short
laugh, that he curtailed with a contrite look when
Lester directed a glower at him.

"Anything else you need to know before I
leave?" Edge asked.

The man went from the archway and rattled
some pans in the kitchen.

"You really kill a man today? For callin' you a
name? Like they say?"

"No," Edge answered Lester, who started to show a sneering grin that was stillborn when the half-breed finished, "For drawing a gun on me after I told him not to."

"Wasn't a man, not really, Lester," the one with green eyes reminded. "Just some kid of a stage guard is what they said down at the saloon."

Fat began to sizzle in a skillet on the stove beyond the arch.

The dog whined that he wanted to get out of the place.

"Animal sounds scared, Lester," the tic muttered toughly, trying to get back on the right side of the top man.

"The guy ain't, Elmer. Not of any kid stage guard, anyways. Nothin' else I need to know, mister. So get that stinkin' mutt outta here. Or is it you that's makin' it so I can't sniff the grub no more?"

They all three sat with their filthy hands resting lightly on the clean cloth that draped the tabletop, supremely confident they could outdraw Edge, whose sheepskin coat was still fastened.

"It's a rat I can smell," the half-breed answered. "You want ventilating, feller?"

And raised the latch as he stooped to the side and allowed the wind to snatch the door from his grasp. It was flung forcefully inwards and slammed against the wall with a sharp crack, followed by the tinkle of falling glass.

From the kitchen came a cry of alarm, and the frightened face of the restauranteur showed at the side of the arch. This as the three men at the table

sat rigidly on their chairs, staring nervously at
Edge, whose slit-eyed gaze had not shifted from
their table since the door had started to swing and
the first hard-driven stream of cold air invaded
the stove heat.

"Trouble is what I smelled!" the Lakeview
lawman snarled, drawing every pair of eyes to
him as he stepped on to the threshold of the restaurant. The wind pushed up one side of his hat
brim and tugged at his open duster to show the
holstered Remington, his right hand draped over
the jutting butt. "And I'm here to stop it before it
gets started."

He looked from the trio of tension-taut men at
the table to the nonchalant Edge and back again,
his cold-pinched face showing an expression that
invited response.

Lester nodded and moved a hand to hold down
the tablecloth being wrenched at by the draft.
"It's my belief, sheriff, that where trouble's concerned, prevention is better than cure. Right
boys?"

"Sure thing, Lester," green eyes supplied.

"Ain't that the truth. Wasn't us broke the man's
door," Elmer added.

"What do you say, mister?" Lester asked of
Edge. "You believe that prevention is better than
cure."

The half-breed had started to go through the
doorway as Sheriff Herman turned sideways to allow him the space. But now he paused briefly to
glance over his shoulder and answer, "Always
have thought the world would be a better place if
some folk's parents had held that belief, feller."

Chapter Twelve

Edge paused again out on the windblown sidewalk and the German shepherd was tensed to respond to a command.

Elmer laughed and the man with green eyes snarled, "Shut up, dummy!"

"What about my busted door?" the restauranteur complained.

The sheriff told him, as he reached in to pull the door closed: "Count your blessin's, Joel Marten. A whole lot more could've been broken."

"But keep cookin' while you're countin', Joel," Lester snapped. "And, Rico, see what you can find to plug the busted glass."

"Damn it, Lester!" the man with green eyes countered miserably. "I ain't no repairman!"

"What you are gettin' to be, Rico, is a pain in the friggin' ass!" the top man of the trio snarled. "Do it!"

Edge had lifted his saddle and bedroll from the angle of the sidewalk and the wall, confident that the immediate threat was past and there was no

need to have his hands free and the scabbarded
Winchester easily accessible. He started along
the sidewalk, eyes cracked to the narrowest of
slits against the wind and the dust motes it carried.

The dog padded along on his left side and the
lawman stayed level on the right. The German
shepherd entirely at ease while the two men remained alert for a sight or sound of the unex-
pected until they were out front of the Timbertops
Livery Stable, which was a block and a half east
of the restaurant on the same side of the street.

Sheriff Herman directed a baleful look back
the way they had come and said, "Guess that
even if you knew what that was about, you
wouldn't tell me?"

"You keep telling everyone how you're not a
man to stick his nose in other people's business,
feller," Edge reminded and nodded his thanks
when the unburdened man opened one of the big
doors and gestured him through.

There were just horses inside the two-story,
hay-lofted livery with stalls around three sides.
Edge's bay gelding and a dozen others for riding
and for hauling. The atmosphere, sharp with the
smell of horse droppings, was cold for men, but
the animals were in enclosed stalls spread with
plenty of warm straw.

"Leo Evers down at the saloon gave me the
word, Edge," the lawman said, leaning his back
against the crack where the two doors were se-
cured at the center of the stable entrance. "Heard
them three guys talkin' with Rita Cornell. Askin'

about you. Her tellin' them how you killed the kid on the stage. And about the big roll you're carryin'."

Edge went to the stall where his gelding was being kept and backed the horse out with soft words of encouragement and a gentle hand. Began to saddle him while the dog moved about the livery, sniffing the many interesting odors contained in the place.

"Don't think you've asked me anything yet, sheriff."

"Don't intend to, Edge. Figure I got me as much trouble as I need with this crazy business between Barny Galton's two sons. And I intend to handle that if it blows up. Kind of blow up there can be between you and them three hard men in the restaurant—well, you should know I wouldn't need to handle it. Not on my own. You and them, we don't normally get your kind in Lakeview. We're way off the beaten track and we ain't got nothin' here for you."

The half-breed lashed his bedroll on behind the saddle and then took out the makings to start a cigarette.

The lawman took a deep breath and went on. "Four in one day is too many. But it could be coincidence and that bunch could've been fixin' to take that bankroll off you. Like I told you before, though, I don't like coincidences."

Edge struck a match and lit the cigarette. On a stream of smoke said, "Something else you told me was that you're not one to beat about the bush."

"You're goin' to ride that horse out of town and off my patch, Edge?"

"Soon as I've bought some supplies for the trail."

Herman shook his head. "Write a list of what you want and I'll see you get it brought here. You can pay the man who brings it."

"Why, sheriff?"

Herman scowled. "Because I don't want any more blood spilled on my patch, that's why. It ain't a coincidence, them being around here at the same time as you, is it?"

Edge pursed his lips as the wind gusted more strongly and there was a flash of lightning from a source a long way off.

"Flush with money because I got paid for killing a man called Al Falcon and shipping his body to Denver, sheriff," the half-breed explained flatly, as a clap of thunder sounded far to the east.

The German shepherd interrupted his investigation of an empty stall and stood stock still —afraid.

"Understand Falcon had a lot of friends and there's a chance that three of them are eating in Joel Marten's place right now."

The scowl on the face of the lawman became more deeply etched in his skin. "Figured somethin' of the sort, mister. In my book, there's nothin' to choose between bounty hunters and the men they hunt."

"Somebody asked you to choose, feller?"

Herman spat at the hard-packed dirt floor in front of his booted feet. "I'm just the one lawman in this town because that's all we need for 99 percent of the time, mister. But when there's any trouble I can't handle, I got almost everyone else who lives in Lakeview to call on for help. Most of them lumbermen, who ain't exactly milksops and who'll fight till the last of them drops if need be to protect what we have here. But I ain't gonna have any of them put their lives on the line in a fight between a bounty hunter and buddies of the last man he had to kill to keep his belly filled."

"Somebody asked that, feller?"

There was another flash of lightning.

"It wasn't just me Leo Evers told about those three and their questions, mister. There was a bunch of men from the lumber camp in the saloon at the same time. Some of them that saw you kill the kid on the stage. Know you are a gunfighter from the way you shaped up to him. Saw the kind them three are too. But they was all ready to go on down to Joel Marten's restaurant and bust all your heads if that was what was called for to stop trouble in Lakeview."

The thunderclap in the wake of the lightning sounded while Herman was speaking and started the German shepherd to whimpering, his eyes staring and his ears pricked. The lawman glanced at the unsettled dog and said in passing: "Barny Galton always said that thunder was all that animal was afraid of."

Edge answered: "A lot of things scare me, feller. But I try not to let them worry me if there's something that has to be done."

Herman stared hard at the half-breed, concerned by the countless implications that could be read into the evenly spoken words.

"Give you an instance," Edge continued in the
same easy manner. "It scares me to think what a
bunch of hard-bitten lumbermen will do to me
afterwards. But that won't keep me from killing
anyone in this town who tries to keep me from
getting out of it before the weather closes in."

Herman's fleshy face carried the grimace for a
moment more, and then became almost impassive
when he said: "All right, mister. Gonna rain is
all. Been threatenin' for a week or more. Reason
you ain't seen no lumber wagons rollin' outta
town. Men worried they'd get bogged down in
this kinda storm. But a man ridin' a horse'll be
okay. Take care in this town, though. Rain, shine,
snow, or heat wave—the weather'll be the least of
your worries if there's shootin' trouble between
you and them other strangers. Started by you."

He raised the latch and had to use force to shift
the outward-opening door against the pressure of
the wind. A flurry of raindrops lashed loudly on
the stable facade and windows, and a brilliant
lightning flash momentarily drove the murkiness
of the afternoon to far distant horizons.

The dog knew the thunder would follow and
was tense and panting, waiting for it—lunged toward the gap at the center of the double doors
when the violent clap cracked across the sky and
vibrated the windows. But Sheriff Herman was
out on the street and the wind had slammed the
door closed behind him a full second before the
terrified animal would have raced through.

"Easy, feller, easy," Edge called across the livery in the wake of the clap and the slam of the
door. While the dog began to pace back and

forth across the securely closed doors, whining his fear of the storm and every now and then venting a snarling bark of frustration that he was trapped.

The half-breed hung the cigarette from a corner of his mouth and led the gelding toward the door, where the German shepherd was abruptly excited. Was down on his haunches now, nose pressed to the center crack, sniffing the many scents of the embryo storm. And also the scent of a man, the sound of whose approach was masked by the howl and buffet of the gusting, rain-streaked wind.

Edge abandoned his grip on the reins of the quiet gelding and made to stoop to catch hold of the frightened dog's rope collar.

But then the sheet lightning exploded brilliance again and the electric crack came just a part of a second later. The German shepherd vented a cry that was eerie in pitch—then was curtailed by a bark of sheer joy when the door was wrenched open. Rain beat inside, to lash at Edge's upturned face. His cigarette was put out and pulped. The dog sprang forward, through the widening gap. And the man who had opened the escape route snarled an obscenity as he was almost knocked over by the animal who bounced off his legs.

A middle-aged man of medium build, hatless but otherwise entirely cloaked in black oilskins.

"Dogs!" he snarled as he stepped over the threshold and leaned against the door he allowed to bang closed at his back. A scowl hard set on his deeply lined, element-burnished face as he ran

both hands through his thick, gray hair to finger
comb rainwater out of it. "Never had no time for
the flea-ridden animals myself. Be two dollars,
mister."

"For losing me my dog?" Edge asked as he
straightened up and turned to the side to spit the
remains of the cigarette off his lips.

"For takin' care of your horse, mister. Stablin',
feedin', and waterin' is two dollars a day here. Or
part of a day. Name's Frank Benson and I'm the
liveryman. Usually hotel guests with horses pay
Polly Webster for the livery service and I collect
from her. But I understand Max didn't make no
charge for—"

"No sweat," Edge cut in on the man. Who had
started to transform his scowl into a frown of anxiety as he watched the half-breed unfasten the but-
tons of the sheepskin coat. But then the former expression was reestablished when he saw the
brown-skinned right hand move to a hip pocket of
the pants and bring out a roll of bills. "You can
ask your town lawman. Wasn't planning on making a run for it. Always do pay my way. Max
wouldn't take my money. Obliged if you'd put two
in the town poorbox, feller?"

Benson accepted the four singles held out to
him and nodded his thanks as he reached through
a slit in the oilskins to put the money in a pocket of
his pants. Then he searched the stable with his
eyes and gave a grunt of satisfaction. Crossed to a
corner stall and took down from a peg a battered
and stained Stetson that hung there. Jammed it on
his head and came back to the doorway.

"Pleasure to do business with you," he said.

"Sorry about the dog. But reckon he'll show up again soon as the lightning and thunder's done with. Here, I'll hold the door for you while you get your mount outside."

He needed to talk louder now, to make himself heard above the din of the strengthening storm, the rain that beat against the walls and roof of the livery sometimes masking the sounds of the wind that drove it.

"Obliged," Edge answered and nodded that he was ready as he took hold of the gelding's bridle.

Frank Benson turned, raised the latch, and leaned forward, head ducked, to fight the door open wide enough for the horse to be led outside.

A man shouted, "Now, damnit!"

Hoofbeats hit the street, just discernible through the storm sounds and the splashing of puddled rainwater kicked up by the pumping legs of the galloping horses.

Sheet lightning flashed and the thunder cracked without a measurable period of time between. Murk that was close to night dark was for a split second changed into a brightness the sun could never match. To show Lester, Rico, and Elmer in stark clarity, crouched low in their saddles as they raced their mounts in a single file along the center of the street. West to east. Each with his right arm held across the front of his chest, hand fisted around the butt of a revolver.

"Benson!" Edge shouted, letting go of the bridle of his horse to turn and reach for the scabbarded Winchester.

The liveryman started to bring up his head, but there was no time for any other voluntary move.

For the lightning flash was gone and he could see
nothing but lancing drops of rain for the moment
before muzzle flashes—mere short-lived streaks
through the sodden gloom—signaled the approach of bullets toward him.

"It ain't—"

Benson was hit and cried out more in surprise
than pain. The gelding took a bullet—gave a
body-shuddering snort as the half-breed slid the
rifle from the scabbard.

"Shit!"

"Keep shootin', he's gotta be—"

Many other voices were raised to roar through
the sounds of the storm and the racing horses. To
merge with and make incomprehensible what the
trio of riders were snarling.

But Lester's order was heard by Rico and Elmer. And all three exploded shots toward the livery doorway again, the spurts of the muzzle
flashes showing as Edge thumbed back the hammer of the Winchester.

But the half-breed was not able to trigger the rifle. Needed to leap to the side as the gelding went
down on the knees of his forelegs and rolled over.
This at the same time as Frank Benson toppled to
the muddy street—and the wind took control of
the door to slam it violently closed—knocking the
man's feet clear of its arcing path on the way.

And so it was into the door timbers that the second volley of bullets buried themselves. To the
accompaniment of a chorus of snarled oaths from
the trio of gunmen. Until their voices were
drowned by a fusillade of gunfire from west of the
livery stable. The bullets blasting from perhaps

half a dozen guns—revolvers triggered blindly into a lashing curtain fo wind-driven rain. The shooting ended in moments by a man who roared an order that this should be so.

Then there followed a pause of stretched seconds during which the wind and the rain seemed to be the only sounds in the world.

The horse sighed and Edge vented a soft curse as he rose from where he had thrown himself to avoid being crushed by the toppling gelding.

Running feet splashed across the liquid mud of the street surface. And several voices were raised, competing to be heard by all and failing to be understood by any.

Edge moved around to the other side of the horse, which was sprawled out on his side. And stooped down to peer at the bloody hole just below the point of the left shoulder. Said softly to the easily breathing animal, "Maybe it's no big thing, feller."

The running had stopped and most of the voices were silent out on the street. Then a fist banged on the livery door and the Lakeview lawman yelled:

"It's Sheriff Herman, Edge! You hurt?"

"No, feller."

"Frank Benson's dead. I'm comin' in, okay?"

"Better if you bring the veterinary in with you, feller. Bastards shot my horse."

The door was fought open against the wind and Herman showed his scowling face in the gap. "One of Lakeview's most popular men is dead and you complain about a shot horse!"

Edge was down on his hands and knees, peer-

ing into the blood-weeping wound to see if the
bullet that made the hole was visible. He shifted
the gaze of his slitted blue eyes for just a moment
to look up at the lawman. Then returned his attention to the wound as he replied: "I paid him the
two bucks I owed him, feller. Like to repay this
horse for what he's done for me. Now, you got a
veterinary in this town, or do I have to start digging for the lead myself?"

He failed to see the bullet and ran a hand con-
solingly over the side of the horse's head before
he rose to his feet, the Winchester canted to his
shoulder.

Herman called out into the rain-lashed street:
"Somebody go bring John Payne here. Got a
horse with a bullet in him!"

"Animal doc's out at the sawmill checkin' company stock!" a man answered.

"Obliged, sheriff," Edge said.

"Eddie, ain't you gonna raise a posse and go
after them murderin' sonsofbitches?" a second
man demanded from outside.

Herman looked over his shoulder again to
snarl, "Just do like I said and get Frank's remains
down to the mortician, uh?" Then he stepped into
the livery and the wind slammed the door behind
him. And he asked grimly, "They just gotta be
buddies of the guy you earned bounty on, don't
they?"

"If I riled them over something else, I don't
know what it could be, sheriff."

A nod. "Haven't got a hope in hell's chance of
trackin' men in this storm." He paused as lightning flashed and waited for the thunder to crack

before he went on: "And won't be easy to pick up on their signs after this weather has blown out. But I don't reckon on the need to go out after them now or later."

He eyed the impassive-faced Edge with a quizzical light in his eyes and the half-breed returned the questioning gaze levelly as he rasped the back of a hand over the bristles on his jaw.

"Maybe they saw me go down and thought I'd been hit. Didn't know I was just getting out from under the falling horse. Whichever, they can't be sure if I'm dead or alive. Only thing they can be sure of is that Benson wasn't me."

"And they'll need to be certain, mister. After takin' so much trouble."

"Guess so, sheriff."

"You always pay your way, mister. You also return favors?"

"I owe you one?"

"They were set to blast you at Joel Marten's restaurant when I showed up. And they'd have got you—three to one like it was. So I reckon I saved your skin, Edge. Least you can do is help me put the arm on them for murderin' Frank Benson."

Edge nodded. "Figure I'll stay around, sheriff."

Herman was curious. "As easy as that?"

"I told them they had to kill me if they aimed guns at me. And they shot my horse while they were trying to do that. They're also to blame for me having to stay in Lakeview and I told you what I'd do to anyone who did that. So your itch to get that three ain't nothing to the one I got, feller."

The scowl spread across the face of the lawman

again and the rasping tone returned to his voice.

"I intend to do it legal, mister. You step across the line for revenge and it'll go bad for you."

Lightning flashed and the pause before the thunder cracked was longer than the last time. But the wind gusted just as strongly and the rain lashed just as hard at the livery.

"Tell you something, sheriff," the half-breed answered as he dropped down to his haunches and began to caress the neck of the shot horse. "If I was the worrying kind, I'd only start to get anxious when things went good for me."

The Lakeview lawman vented a harsh snort of disgust as he reached for the door latch and growled, "Savin' my sympathy for Frank Benson's widow, mister."

He went out then and allowed the wind to slam the door closed. While Edge expressed perplexity for stretched seconds as he continued to stroke the gelding and asked:

"Shit, did that sound like I was fishing for pity, feller?"

The horse paid no attention and the man shook his head reflectively. Then, just for a moment, there was a deep sadness in the set of the cruel mouth line and the glinting slits of the ice-blue eyes. When he glanced at the crack where the two doors met. And saw in his mind's eye a vivid image of the German shepherd when he lunged out of the livery. Then grinned, with an infrequent warmth in his eyes, when he heard a familiar whine.

Rose from comforting the unresponsive horse to go to the door and inch it open. But there was no dog out in the teeming rain. And he realized the sound he thought had been made by an uneasy dog was in fact the squeak from the swinging sign that jutted out above the livery stable entrance.

A voice said from the right: "Men have come in from the lumber camps, mister. So the animal doc should be here soon."

Edge cracked the door wider to get his head through the gap. And saw a tall man leaning against the closed door. Wearing hooded black oilskins that the wind pressed hard to his body, contouring his muscular frame. He held a rifle canted across his chest—gripping it very tightly.

"Thought I heard the dog out here."

"Nah," the man assured. "Scared dog runs for home. I bet that dog's gone all the way back to old Barny Galton's claim. I bet you."

"Obliged."

"I know dogs, mister. Kept them all my life. And I know what that animal belonged to old Barny Galton is like."

"Obliged," Edge told him again. "You standing guard out there?"

Sheet lightning hit the teeming murk and the half-breed was able in the moment of brilliant illumination to see that the man in the black oilskins was not alone on the street. For outside every building there was at least one other man posted as a sentry—some in the pouring rain and others standing in the shelter of sidewalk or stoop awnings. Some armed with rifles at the ready. Others with gunbelts slung around their waists.

"Me and the whole town, mister," the man out

front of the livery said after the thunder had
rolled far in the distant west. "Like I said, most
men are in from the lumber camps, on account of
the storm callin' an early halt to the day's work.
Them that didn't see Frank Benson with the two
holes in his head, they heard about it. And everyone's real eager to help out when a good man like
Frank Benson gets dead that way."

"The sheriff say anything to you and the others
about me, feller?"

"Just that you're the bait, mister."

"Obliged."

"You're welcome."

Edge withdrew into the stable and allowed the
wind to slam the door closed. The wounded gelding, which did not seem to be in too much discomfort, looked dolefully up at the man after he
had dropped to his haunches again—but this time
to take a carton of shells for the Winchester out of
a saddlebag. And to fix the roll of bills from his
hip pocket under the bridle noseband.

"Help's on its way to you, feller," the half-
breed told the animal in a soothing tone. "Need to
go get that storm-crazy dog before he gets his
head blown off by that Galton woman."

He rose and checked over the other horses in
the livery, and selected a big chestnut mare.
Took the gear off a peg at the front of her stall and
saddled and bridled her. Then led her to the stable entrance, needing to carry his rifle because
there was no scabbard fixed to the saddle.

He pushed the door wide open and hooked it to
remain so, head ducked into the rain-soaked

wind and ignoring the man in the black oilskins.
Who seemed too startled to speak as he watched
Edge fix open the door. Then demanded, "What
the hell, mister?"

"You're the man I saw about a dog, feller. Need
to go see the dog now."

"But—"

"Don't aim the rifle at him or he'll kill you, Joe,"
Sheriff Herman growled as he came out of the bil-
lowing curtain of rain with another man at his
side.

This just as the lightning flashed once more, to
illuminate the scene out front of the livery. Which
caused a number of the men on both sides of the
street to advance from their sentry positions.

"This is John Payne, the vet who'll take a look at
your horse, Edge," the sheriff said as a dozen or
so men closed in on the front of the stable. This as
the thunder crackled and rolled.

All, save for Herman and Payne, fingered their
guns. The sheriff had his hands deep in the pockets of his sodden duster, while the overcoated vet-
erinarian held a heavy bag with both hands.

"Glad he'll be in good hands, feller," the half-
breed said with a nod to the young and nervous-
looking animal doctor, as he led the mare out into
the slightly easing storm.

"That's Frank Benson's horse you're stealin',
mister," Herman growled as Payne went quickly
and with a sigh of relief into the shelter of the livery.

"Nah, it's the mare, Eddie," Joe pointed out.
"Mary's horse."

"Reckon stealin' from a new widow is maybe even worse than stealin' from the new dead," Herman answered.

"Hey, there's a whole bundle of money in here," Payne called. "Has to be two hundred dollars at least, I'd say."

"For your services," Edge said into the stable. Then looked toward the lawman as he swung up astride the mare. "And a deposit against me bringing the horse back."

There were some growls of discontent among the group of armed lumbermen, which were curtailed when the sheriff snapped:

"You've got one heck of a nerve, Edge!"

"Yeah, feller."

"You said you'd stick around."

"After I've found the dog, I'll be back."

"I told him the dog'd be back at old Barny Galton's claim, Eddie," Joe explained, ready to be apologetic if it was the wrong thing to have said.

"I'm gettin' to be friggin' weary of you and that animal, mister!" Herman snarled.

"So why don't you go and bed down for a while, sheriff," the half-breed answered evenly as he heeled the mare slowly forward and with a tug of the reins headed him eastward. "Best thing for a man that's dog tired."

Chapter Thirteen

Edge was grim faced as he rode the chestnut mare along the storm-lashed street. Not because he was aware of the possibility that the Lakeview lawman might feel an irresistible impulse to try to stop the departure. Instead, his dour mood was dictated by his feelings for the big German shepherd as he visualized the dog—sodden and shivering with cold and fear—arriving on the familiar territory of the claim across the lake in search of a comforting place to shelter from the storm. Perhaps so crazed with irrational terror of the thunder that his canine brain was unable to retain memories of the recent past. So he would prowl the claim in search of Barny Galton, who —during many other storms—had maybe known how to calm the dog.

Scratching and howling at the door of the cabin. Which was thrown open to reveal the substantial form of Janet Galton standing on the threshold. Her brain swamped by a vivid memory of the dog when it was poised to attack. This as she aimed the double-barrel shotgun at the pa-

thetically afraid animal. And squeezed both trig-
gers.

Edge was off the end of the street and riding
along the spur that joined the main trail out of
Lakeview. Out of sight of Eddie Herman and the
lumbermen who were determined to avenge the
tragic killing of Frank Benson. The half-breed
made a conscious effort to rid his mind of the image of the dog's death, and to concentrate his attention on following the trail in the near dark of
the stormy afternoon.

It could well be that the three revenge-eager
gunmen were waiting in the timber somewhere
just off the trail he rode. Expecting a posse to
come after them despite the bad weather. With or
without Edge along. Ready to ambush the group
if he was among the riders, or to let them pass and
backtrack to Lakeview if he wasn't. Hardly able to
believe his stupidity and their luck when he appeared entirely alone.

The pace had to be slow along the trail turned
by the rain into an unmoving river of mud, and
the half-breed needed constantly to check his anger and frustration. He found it increasingly difficult to keep his mind uncluttered by futile imag-
inings concerning the fate of the dog who had
shared his life for so short a time.

Perhaps the German shepherd had never made
it back to the claim. Was off the trail behind Edge
now. Shot dead or worse—injured and dying—by
the three friends of Al Falcon who had mistaken
his fear of the storm for an intent to attack as the
dog sprang out of the night.

Or had reached the claim. Where Janet Galton

and her husband were no longer the only potential dangers. Lee Galton was over there on the other side of Mirror Lake now. With Max Webster and the two old-timers and two kids who Galton had managed to get to ride with him around to the claim. Any one of them might mistake the dog's intent and blast a bullet into the animal.

Difficult to stem the rising tide of such useless thoughts, but not impossible. And he was alert enough to know when he was nearing the point where the track leading to the claim cut off the main trail. He steered the mare to the right side of the trail, peering through the slanting rain in search of the gap in the timber with the ancient sign that warned strangers to keep away.

Full night was clamped over this area of the Montana Rockies by then and the electric storm was long gone beyond the high ridges to the west. But the wind blew just as hard as ever, veering and gusting, bitingly cold and heavy with icy raindrops.

When Edge reached the cutoff track to the south side of the lake, though, he felt no colder or wetter than when he rode out of town. For over just the block or so from the livery to the open trail, without him being aware of it, the storm had unleashed the full weight of its discomfort on him. And he continued to be oblivious to the sodden touch of his clothing to his skin and the chill blast of needling rain against his face and hands as he paused beside the leaning sign with the burnt lettering along the cross member. This as he became tensed to meet potential danger—sensing the proximity of somebody else on the trail he had just covered. Turning his horse to face back that way, narrowed eyes straining to see who was there. Knowing that he would fail to hear anything short of a gunshot against the beat of rain and the swish of the wind through the timber.

A horse and rider. The rider hunched in the saddle, head bent to protect the face from the lash of the wind-driven rain. The sides of the head protected by a scarf that came out from under the brim of a Stetson to be tied under his chin. A black oilskin slicker draping the frame. No gun in sight, so Edge kept the barrel of the Winchester resting lightly across the horn of his saddle, aimed into the trees, as he allowed the tension to drain out of him.

"Something else I can't do for you, Miss Webster?" he asked.

She had sensed his nearness and snapped her head a part of a second before he spoke. And while he voiced the sardonic comment she gasped and reined in her mount. Then, her soured face altered its set from a grimace of fear to a look of entreaty.

"They said you were going out to that crazy old man's claim, Mr. Edge."

"They didn't lie."

"I'm worried about Max."

"He's close to seven feet tall, I figure. Big enough to look after himself."

She looked about to snap an angry retort, but then checked the impulse and continued in the same tone as before. "You must know Max isn't the brightest man in the world, Mr. Edge. And didn't you see the others that went with him from town? Old Kitteridge and Sam Nelson, who're close to being senile. And them two Hall boys, who'd flap their arms and try to fly off a mountain-top if you offered them ten cents to do it."

"Claim's down this trail," the half-breed said with a gesture of the rifle.

"I know it, mister. And so does every one else from Lakeview. Know, too, that there ain't nothin' at the end of it but a lousy shack and a lot of holes in the ground. And what that crazy old Barny Galton wrote in the letters to his boys was so much eyewash, to get them to come out and see him before he died."

"I'm hopeful there's a dog at the end of the trail," Edge told her and tugged on the reins of the mare as he touched his heels to her flanks. He started the horse down the sidetrack that crossed the timber slope toward the east shore of Mirror Lake.

"Wait for me!" the woman cried, and within a few moments had brought her mount up along-side that of the half-breed. Said after a lengthy pause, "There isn't, you know."

"What, Miss Webster?"

"Any gold at the claim."

"If you say so. I say that I'm just going back there to look for the dog."

He sensed her eyes peering at his profile as they reached the foot of the slope, and the sound of the wind-whipped waters of the lake hitting the shore made conversation in the storm even harder.

"Not a man like you!" she yelled. "I just can't believe you'd go to this much trouble over a dog!"

"Lady, I don't give a shit what you believe!" Edge shouted back.

And then groaned with a mixture of anger and disappointment when a man ride his horse out from behind a rock on the lakeshore and bellowed:

"You better friggin' believe me and my partners got you covered, you bushwhackin' bastard!"

It was Elmer, the man Rico had called dummy. Grinning in triumph through the rain as he leveled his handgun at Edge as the half-breed and the woman reined their horses to a halt some ten feet away from where Elmer sat his mount.

Polly Webster said in a choked tone, "Oh, my God!"

Elmer, his grin getting even broader, taunted, "He ain't gonna help no one rides with this bastard!"

Edge turned his head fractionally to the left and raked his glinting eyes along their sockets to see Lester and Rico emerge from the trees. Also with guns drawn and leveled to the sides of their mounts' necks.

"Right, you old hag!" Lester blurted gleefully. "You ain't worth keepin' alive for a little fun! Lookin' like you do, I reckon it's been so long since that last time, it's grown over."

"If there was ever a first time with her, Lester!" Elmer yelled, and laughed harshly.

Rico, the degree of his grim-faced seriousness

stressed by the glee of the others, said harshly, "Tip that rifle off your saddle, Edge."

He and the top man of the three had halted their horses at the side of the trail, some six feet to the left of where Edge sat his mare—left hand on the reins while the right was fisted around the frame of the uncocked Winchester, the muzzle of which was aimed at the tree trunk between Rico and Lester.

"Lady's like the feller you killed back at Lakeview," Edge said, head half turned now to allow his eyes to see all three men as clearly as possible through the wind-slanted rain. "An innocent party. Let her go and—"

"Innocent party is right, Edge," Elmer blurted and laughed loudly. "With the kinda sourpuss she's got, innocent is what she has to be! Ain't that so, Lester?"

The man's laughter together with the crash of lake water against the shore, the moan of the wind through the trees, and the splatter of rain on everything, covered the metallic clicks of the rifle's hammer being thumbed back.

"Sure, Elmer," Lester answered in an abruptly harsh tone. "So why don't you put the old hag outta her misery. Then we can make this bushwhackin' bastard pay for what he done to Al back in Kansas."

"Please, no!" the woman shrieked.

The half-breed experienced—not for the first dangerous moment in a life largely lived on the borderline between survival and violent death— a sense of the unreal that had the quality of a dream. In which he could not be certain of anything except his own actions and reactions to what might or might not have been actually heard or seen.

Thus, he could not be sure that in the instant before Polly Webster pleaded for her life, he actually did hear a familiar growling sound. To his left and behind him .

He was certain that unless he retaliated or discarded his rifle, he would die from a bullet exploded by Rico's gun. Certain that Rico was the one who was most distrustful of his earnest attitude, which Lester was beginning to find infectious.

To allow the rifle to fall to the muddy track was to signal the death of the woman by the revolver in Elmer's hand. And to invite for himself a much harder way to die than by a gunshot.

He heard the woman catch her breath as she saw Elmer's arm reach toward her, the hand at its end fisted around the butt of his Colt.

Saw Elmer's action and flicked his eyes along their sockets between the narrowest of lids and vented a sigh, as if resigned to inevitable death.

Lester began to curl back his lips in a grin again, convinced of the truth of this.

While Rico remained tensely suspicious of the half-breed, who said evenly:

"Good a night as any to die. When it's raining frogs and dogs."

Elmer laughed at the error.

Rico started, "Quit the talk and tip that Win—"

Lester corrected, "Friggin' cats and dogs, you bushwha—"

It was Rico's aggressive tone of voice that had

stirred the German shepherd. And the younger man was closer to the dog when Lester spoke the word guaranteed to unleash the canine fury.

Abruptly the dreamlike quality of a partially unreal world was gone.

The dog lunged up from the brush and Rico threw himself away from the animal, sideways off his horse. Too intent upon getting out of range of the extended claws and the exposed fangs to think about the Colt in his hand.

Lester snapped his head to the side to stare at Rico and the dog and then made to bring his suddenly rage-filled gaze back to locate the half-breed.

Edge elevated the barrel of the rifle and moved it fractionally forward. Squeezed the trigger and did not watch as the bullet drilled into Lester's chest, from a range that was close enough with a high-velocity rifle for the shell to jerk the victim violently backwards with the force of impact.

This at the same time that Rico came voluntarily clear of his saddle, but watching the dog instead of where he was going. So crashed his head into the side of the tree that grew tall and straight between his own mount and that of the dying Lester. Hit the trunk hard and awkwardly enough for the collision to break his neck with a sickening sound of snapping bone.

The snarls and barks of the maddened dog disturbed all five horses on the lakeside trail the mount of Elmer affected no more nor less than the others. But the surviving member of the trio of Al Falcon's friends was in the grip of fear of his own. Terrified by the abrupt turnabout of a situation in

which—a moment earlier—he and his partners
had appeared unassailable. And mixed in with
the fear of what was happening was a fury that it
had been allowed to happen.

During this flurry of violent action, Polly Webster sat rigidly erect in the saddle of her head-
tossing, ground-scratching mount, her eyes
squeezed tightly closed and hands pressed over
her ears. Her lips were pulled wide in a piercing
scream and, with her hands covering her ears instead of gripping the reins, the inevitable happened. When the horse reared in panic, and she
was tossed backwards from the saddle to crash to
the rain-softened trail.

Elmer had fired once at Edge but it was an in-
stinctive shot, his aim further spoiled by the
movement of his mount. The bullet going high
and wide out across the lake.

Now he triggered a second bullet from the
Colt. His horse four footed and his stretched arm
held rock steady. But the grin of triumph that had
began to spread across his cold-pinched, rain-
water-run face started to alter into a look of de-
spair. Which took on a frozen quality at the moment he fired his gun.

For an instant of muzzle flash just preceded the
report from his revolver. Down at the right hip of
the half-breed and at side of the mare's neck as it,
too, became four footed.

Elmer knew he had failed. Failed worse than
Lester and Rico, who had been surprised by the
way the dog sprang out of nowhere. While Edge
had the rifle aimed in their direction. So, as the
dog was going for Rico and the man was blasting

at Lester, he should have plugged Edge. Instead
of which, he wasted a fatal length of time staring
at his dying partners and then was distracted by
the old sourpuss making that awful row. Dummy
was right. He forgave Rico for calling him that all
the time. And started to hate that cocksure Lester
for going against what Rico said. Rico was for all
three of them blasting at Edge from out of the
darkness. Killing him before he knew what had
hit him. But no, Lester had said they should capture him and give him hell for a long time. Some
Apache torture Lester and Al Falcon had come
across way back.

The thoughts came and went in the mind of
Elmer quicker than the lightning flashes of the
earlier part of the storm. A thousand of them, it
seemed, in the time it took for the bullet to explode from the muzzle of the rifle and blast an entrance into the center of his forehead. And he was
dead. Tumbling backwards off his horse as Edge
hurled himself sideways off his.

The half-breed's mind was as devoid of thought
as his face was lacking in expression during the
moments of time separating the death of Lester
and the killing of Elmer.

This as he angled the Winchester skywards,
pressing the stock against his thigh while his right
hand flicked forward and was snapped back to
pump the lever action. The horse reared and he
fought to regain control of her with a left hand on
the reins. Rico and Lester were already off their
mounts by then and the tone of Polly Webster's
scream had changed as she began to slide from
her saddle. But the slitted blue eyes under the

hooded lids concentrated to the exclusion of all else on Elmer's head—as the man stared in horror at his partners with the same expression at the shrieking woman, and then started to grin.

The younger man's mount was marginally quicker in thudding down on to all four hooves. But the half-breed elected to fire the rifle the moment his target was steady rather than to wait until the mare was. And started to power out of the saddle an instant after he triggered the shot from the Winchester in the one-handed grip. An instant later saw the grin of Elmer's face start to change and saw, also, on the periphery of his vision, the muzzle flash of the Colt. And knew with a briefly experienced sense of cold-hearted triumph that this shot from the revolver would be as ineffective as the one exploded while the man's horse was at the top of its rear.

Then the half-breed fell on something softer than the muddy surface of the trail and heard Polly Webster scream again after a moment's pause. He rolled off of her, on to his knees, and used the Winchester as a lever to get to his feet. Peered down at the woman venting the shrill sound and saw that she was sprawled out on her back with her eyes still screwed shut, her hands over her ears, and her mouth wide open.

"Lady!" he snarled. But no spoken word could ever be loud enough to penetrate into the world of terror that enclosed her. So he straddled her, leaned down, and swung a vicious backhanded slap into her left cheek. And her hands flew away from her ears as her head rocked to the side. The scream was curtailed by a gasp. She rolled her head straight again and now her eyes were wide open—showing the same brand of terror that contorted the rest of her features—as she stared up at Edge.

"They're dead and we're alive, Miss Webster!" he shouted at her and was abruptly aware that his voice was too loud. Listened to the verbal silence while the woman flapped her lips without speaking, and heard the rain falling but not the wind blowing. Also heard a sound alien to the storm that he could not quite identify. Said without shouting: "You took a fall is all, lady. And I had a crush on you for a while. Nothing to get excited about."

He swung away from her, trying to think what the sound could be that came from the side of the trail away from the lake. Where the still teeming rain and the cluster of now calm horses obstructed his view.

"Oh, my God, I was sure the end was near for me!" Polly Webster rasped as she struggled painfully to get to her feet—needing to roll over on to her belly and raise herself on to all fours to achieve this.

"It was near, lady," Edge confirmed as he used his free hand to ease a horse out of his path. "But I didn't rise to the occasion and so you didn't have it in you."

"What on earth are you talking—oh, crazy is right about you! Making stupid dirty-minded jokes at a time like—my God, the dog is . . ."

She had come across the trail to stand beside Edge among the horses. Her tone of voice altering each time she allowed a sentence to hang unfinished. Until she was in a position to see what he could and gagged on a tide of rising bile.

Lester was spread-eagled on his back to one side of a Douglas fir tree—no more nauseating a sight than the corpse of Elmer sprawled out beside the rock on the other side of the trail.

It was Rico who had died in the most sickening way, having flung himself unwittingly headfirst into the tree to escape the attacking lunge of the German shepherd. A man with a thin skull who hit the tree too hard. So that his head was split open and its liquid contents spilled out. To stain the tree trunk and the exposed root upon which Rico's head and arms lay in death.

A gruesome enough sight in itself. But the horror of the scene was expanded beyond the bounds of what the woman could stomach by the actions of the dog. Who lay on his belly with his paws extended to hold the dead head of the man still. While he rhythmically lapped at the fluids which continued to ooze from the open skull.

Polly Webster retched, but managed to fight the rising sickness back down her throat as she swung away from the scene. And blurted, "The dog's a monster!"

Then she sank to her hands and knees again in the middle of the trail, and emptied her stomach of everything she had eaten that day.

The dog interrupted his feeding on the contents of a human head and started to growl.

"Easy, feller," Edge murmured.

And now the dog rose, turned from the corpse, and padded toward the half-breed, licking his lips. Sat down close to the man's left leg.

The woman finished being noisily sick and demanded between sobs: "You must put down the creature! It's only one step removed from a wolf and it has developed a taste for human remains!"

"I don't know, lady," Edge said evenly as he stroked the ears of the German shepherd and the dog whimpered softly.

"You saw it with your own eyes, man!" Polly Webster said harshly as she rose to her feet.

Edge shifted his gaze from the man at the base of the tree to the gore-smeared trunk that had caused his death. And whispered against the less obtrusive sound of the slackening rain, "Far as that feller was concerned, lady, it seems to me the bark was worse than the bite."

Chapter Fourteen

The dog remained within a few feet of Edge as the half-breed led the chestnut mare from out of the cluster of horses, and quickly checked that the animal had not sustained any leg injuries during the melee. Then the German shepherd took up his usual position close to the mare's left hind leg after the half-breed had swung up astride the saddle.

The woman watched with eyes that were still wide with remembered terror and horror; coughing and sobbing as she rubbed vigorously at her mouth and chin with a coat sleeve to remove the final remnants of her sickness.

And all the time the rain was easing and the visibilty was lengthening as low cloud moved off in the wake of the electric storm and the high cloud thinned and straggled. But the the Rocky Mountain air got colder as the night advanced and the lights of the town's waterfront street could be seen across Mirror Lake before the moon showed pale through the clouds.

"You're not going to do it, are you?"

"Do what, lady?" Edge countered in an even tone.

"Put down that dog?"

"My business, lady."

"My God, you're always ready to kill a man just like that!" She tried to click her finger and thumb but the skin was too wet for a sound to be made. "Yet you cringe at the thought of putting down a mere dog."

"Lady."

"Yes?"

"I been known to kill women, too."

"Go to hell!" she flung back at him.

"It's a hot idea for a cold night," he muttered and heeled the mare forward. The dog sprang up off his haunches and began to trot along in the wake of rider and mount.

There was just a drizzle drifting out of the sky now, and for the fifteen or so seconds it took for the air to become totally void of rain, Polly Webster watched in a state of rage, the man and his horse and dog moving along the lakeshore. Unable to consider anything other than the revulsion she felt for the dog and its owner.

Until she abruptly realized that Edge was riding south—toward the claim instead of backtracking to town. And her experience with evil on the lakeshore was consigned to a dark recess of her memory as she recalled the desperate errand that had drawn her out into the timber this night.

She hurriedly remounted her horse, taking care to avoid looking at any of the dead men. Then moved off after Edge, but made no attempt to close the gap on him. Despite her reawakened

concern for the fate of her brother, still gleaming
brightly in her mind was an image of the vicious
expression on the face of the man called Edge
during their final exchange. When, Polly Webster was absolutely certain, she had never been
closer to death. And in an immeasurably short
part of a second, the man had switched from one
side to the other of the narrowest of dividing
lines. To rasp a cynical joke about hell instead of
blasting her into it.

Two hundred and fifty yards ahead of the
woman who he knew was trailing him, Edge was
equally well aware of how close he had come to
killing Polly Webster. Which would have been a
bad thing to do, a hard action to live with.

For she had spoken nothing but the truth and
nobody deserved to die for doing that. While the
person responsible for such a killing deserved the
worst that a bad future could hold.

But had the dog not played a part in the violence back on the trail, there would not have
been any kind of future for Edge or the woman.
And before that, in the restaurant, the presence
of the dog had aroused enough interest in the
three gunmen to keep them from blasting at Edge
before the Lakeview sheriff made his play and
took the heat out of the situation.

These dangerous incidents apart, the big German shepherd had still done enough to more than
earn from the half-breed whatever it was that had
almost led to the wanton murder of the hapless
Polly Webster. By the simple process of doing no
more than he was doing now as they rounded the
southern tip of the arm of lake and started back

northward—by being there and asking no more than to be there.

"Shit!" Edge rasped aloud, and spat to the trail side as he reflected that no human companion—male or female—could ever be so undemanding.

The woman was directly opposite him across the narrow stretch of lake and she called.

"Did you say something, Mr. Edge?"

"Just shit, lady!" he answered.

"You're disgusting!"

"Yeah," he growled in a rasping whisper. "It's difficult to see how anyone can take to me, ain't it?"

The dog gave a sharp half bark that carried no note of alarm. And when Edge glanced down at him he saw the mouth was partly open, the tongue lolling out, the fangs and eyes shining brightly in the moonlight—in an expression of canine delight that was matched by the vigorous waving of the tail.

"I know, feller," the half-breed said in a soothingly even tone. "And I think you're pretty terrific too. Except for your taste in food."

Yet again, the German shepherd made it seem as if he understood complex human speech—whined and set his ears back along his head. A sad expression entered his eyes to convey a look of abject contrition, which, despite all else, drew a grin across the face of the man as he murmured:

"That's right, feller. It's a dog-eat-dog world we're living in. Eating people is wrong, even when they happen to be sonsofbitches."

Chapter Fifteen

The man called Edge shot the dog with no name.

The grin wiped from his face a moment after he squeezed the trigger of the rifle he had tilted down off the saddle and angled back across his left thigh. By which time the German shepherd was blind in death, the animal eyes showing total trust in the apparent good humor of the man until the bullet smashing into the head between the eyes abruptly ended every sensation.

The man felt a numbness that had to bear some resemblance to the emptiness of death as he instinctively worked to bring the gunshot-spooked horse back under control while his mind was filled with a rapidly changing series of images of the dog in the quieter times since the first violent meeting between man and animal. More good times than bad, especially during those contented days and nights at the claim.

The mare was calm now and Edge swung down from the saddle. Leaned his rifle against a tree. He had no bedroll blankets so shrugged out of his sheepskin coat and used this as a shroud for the dog, who lay on his side, tail and legs extended and head covered with blood. Stooped to drape the coat over the carcass. Then rose with an easy strength to lift the considerable weight and rest it across the saddle on the mare.

There had been no bad times until other people showed up—the Galtons at the claim. And the bad times had increased almost in proportion to the number of people the man and dog came across in town.

"It's for the best, Mr. Edge," Polly Webster said in a melancholy tone as she reined in her horse a few yards off from where the half-breed was returning to his after retrieving his rifle. "You'd be constantly worried when next the creature's liking for human flesh caused you to—"

"Get your own mind back down between your legs and stop trying to read mine, lady," Edge cut in on her coldly as he canted the Winchester to his left shoulder and started to lead the mare along the trail with his right hand on the bridle.

The woman gasped, then snarled, "Digusting is right!"

Did not start out in the wake of Edge again until he was perhaps fifty yards ahead. And drawing close to where the trail angled away from the shore of the lake and began to climb the timber-clad slope to the top of the promontory's landward end.

The half-breed was aware of exactly where he was as he trudged along the muddy track, feeling no colder without the rain-sodden coat on his back than when he wore it. And, but for a blurred mental picture of the upturned head of the German shepherd a moment before he shot him, the mind of the man was uncluttered by memories. A blurred image that was a true one, since the reality had been lacking in sharpness . . .

Then even this was gone and that part of his mind not concerned with monitoring the signals from the eyes, ears, and sixth sense for danger was determinedly concentrated upon what he intended to do at the top of the slope he was climbing.

"Mr. Edge, do you consider it wise to approach so openly?" Polly Webster asked with a strong note of unease in her voice. Speaking from just a few yards behind the half-breed, having closed the gap with nervous glances in every direction as the slope began. And the trees grew close to both sides of the track, their foliage all but blotting out the light of the moon.

"How's that, lady?"

"It could be dangerous for us if somebody misinterprets our reason for being here."

"I'm not a thief in the night, lady," he answered, speaking at a normal conversational level that sounded close to shouting in contrast with the woman's rasping whispers. "Could be mistaken for one if I approached like one."

"I'd like to know what you are here for!" she countered sourly.

"You're not the only one, sis!" the towering Max Webster growled.

"And nobody invited you either!" the pretty-faced, stout-bodied Janet Galton added in a similarly harsh tone.

They stepped out of the timber on either side

of the trail as Edge leading his horse with the
mounted woman immediately behind the mare
reached the top of the rise. Where the track gave
on to the clearing with the log cabin as its center.
The tall man and the fat woman both warmly
garbed against the cold bite of the night air. He
with a rifle and she with the bullet-nicked shotgun. Each held in gloved hands across the base of
their bellies—ready to be swung and raised to
augment the threats implicit in the scowling
faces.

"Max!" Polly Webster blurted joyfully. "Thank
God you're all right!"

"I told her you were big enough to take care of
yourself, feller," Edge said as he halted, not
needing to tighten his grip around the frame of
the Winchester. For he had just the right kind of
hold on the rifle and had shifted his thumb to the
hammer when he first suspected there were
guards at the way in to the clearing.

"I was worried, that's all, Max," the sister of the
suddenly embarrassed-looking man assured.

"Like I am about you coming back to the claim,
mister!" the Galton woman snapped, her eyes
flicking this way and that. "And where's that
brute of an animal that almost—"

"Dead, ma'am," Edge cut in on the untrusting
woman as he completed making a cursory survey
of the brightly moonlit clearing. And became the
subject of a survey himself, by the group of men
who gathered at a front corner of the cabin, close
to where the rented buggy was parked.

The horse that had pulled the rig from Lakeview and the mounts of the men who had ridden

from town were hobbled out back of the cabin.

"Who is it?" Lee Galton yelled, the tone of his voice expressing angry impatience.

"Edge!" the bearded brother's sister-in-law called back, making the name sound like an obscenity.

"And my sister Polly!" Max added.

"Plus a dead dog," Edge added, a hint of impatience in his voice.

He tugged on the bridle of the mare and started toward the abruptly startled Janet Galton and Max Webster. Then added, as the pair looked at each other for a first move to follow, "Who I've brought home to bury."

"What?" the fat woman gasped, but stepped aside.

"Sis?" the towering Webster queried with a puzzled frown and also moved out of the half-breed's path.

Edge's contribution had not been spoken loudly enough to carry to the Galton brothers and four Lakeview citizens grouped at the corner of the cabin.

The bearded and battered-faced Lee demanded, "What's goin' on here?"

Then the shorter, thinner spectacle-wearing Ralph started, "You told us you agreed to relinquish all rights to my father's—"

His wife interrupted, "He says he's only here to bury the dog, Ralph!"

There was a sudden babble of talk among the six strong group beside the cabin. The sense of what was being said not carrying to the ears of Edge, but he was able to detect the note of incredulity in the competing voices. Then, as he veered to the left to go around the neglected vegetable patch and behind the cabin, voices were raised.

"We heard shootin'!"

"Like a damn battle at first!"

"Way over the east side of the lake!"

"Then a shot close by!"

"Edge, damnit, you can't just—"

"He's got somethin' wrapped in a cover over his saddle!"

The half-breed ignored the actual and the implied questions as he made directly for the elongated mound with the rock-formed cross on it over by the outcrop on the far side of the clearing.

Polly Webster rode her horse into the clearing and on to the once carefully cultivated area of land.

"Hey!" Janet Galton snapped.

"Polly, you better take care—" Max started.

"The crazy man means what he says!" the woman cut in on the many voices as she halted her mount. "His dog ran away in the storm and he came after it. Three men left town in a hurry as well. After they shot and killed Frank Benson while they were tryin' to shoot Edge. The first gunfire you heard . . ."

Polly Webster continued to give her startled audience an account of the events that led to she and Edge arriving at the claim. While the half-breed commenced the chore he had set himself. After first hitching the mare to a clump of brush and relieving her of the burden of the dead dog.

He noticed indifferently that after the body of Barny Galton had been exhumed to check on the manner of his death, his son had made a neat job of reburying the corpse and replacing the cross of stones.

The shovel that had been used for the opening and refilling of the grave had been discarded nearby and Edge used this to dig a hole for the dog alongside the last resting place of his one-time master.

After a chorus of questions when Polly Webster had finished, the volume of voices was lowered and Edge was unable to understand what was being said as he worked steadily at digging the grave for the dog. Then it was as if he was alone in the clearing, when everyone else was in the cabin, its thick log walls totally muting whatever exchanges took place inside.

Until, when he had almost dug down as deeply as was necessary, he heard heavy footfalls on the rain-soddened ground as counterpoint to the thud of the shovel into the dirt. And looked up to see Max Webster approaching him. The big-built man no longer carried the rifle. The half-breed continued with the grave.

"I don't think it's crazy, you doin' this," Webster said as he halted a few feet off from the grave.

"So I'm not touched, feller," the half-breed answered as he tossed a final shovelful of earth out of the four-foot-deep, elongated hole. And climbed up out from it. Pushed the blade of the shovel into the heap of displaced earth and took the makings from a shirt pocket.

Webster was briefly puzzled by the response,

then shrugged his shoulders. "We're the crazy ones, sir. Them Galtons and us Lakeview people that come out here with Lee. There ain't nothin' here on old Barny's place worth the ride around the lake for."

"You came around the lake, feller," Edge reminded as he rolled the paper around the tobacco.

Webster grimaced. "Yeah. Me and the Hall boys. Sam Nelson and Billy Kitteridge. With not the brains and good sense of one man spread around all five of us."

"Somebody else said something like that," Edge answered and lit the cigarette with a match struck on the butt of his holstered Colt.

"We all know we ain't the smartest," Max Webster said flatly. "And I guess that Lee Galton was told what a bunch of dumb clucks we are. By folks that had more sense than to pay any attention to what was in the letter old Barny wrote him."

Edge cupped his hands around the end of the cigarette as he drew against it, deriving a little warmth from the red-hot tobacco leaves.

"Same letter Barny wrote to Ralph we found out after we got here," Webster went on, eager to talk and uncaring that he had such an unresponsive audience of one. "Didn't have no trouble like Lee did when his brother and Mrs. Galton jumped him the first time. They couldn't do nothin' like that against six of us. So Lee and Ralph and Mrs. Galton they put their heads together and decided to throw in together. Which is the way old Barny wanted it to be."

"What are you and others from town in for?"

Edge asked as the expression on the face of the big man seemed to plead for encouragement to go on.

Now Webster briefly smiled as he patted the area of his hip pocket.

"Lee gave us twenty dollars each to ride out here with him. And there's the promise of the rest to make it up to a hundred when his inheritance is found. His and Ralph's inheritance, that is."

"Which you don't figure is here, Max?" the half-breed said indifferently as he arced the partly smoked cigarette into the sodden timber and went to where the coat-wrapped carcass of the dog lay.

"Look at it this way, sir," Webster replied quickly, obviously pleased to be arousing some degree of interest in Edge now. "Old Barny Galton worked this claim for almost as long as anyone can recall. Lived over here in that shack like a hermit. Grew and shot most of what he ate. When he did come to Lakeview, it was to change a little bit of gold dust into money at the bank and buy some trifle he wanted."

Edge considered only briefly reclaiming his sheepskin coat. But decided against it and kept the carcass of the German shepherd wrapped in it as he dropped to his haunches to lower the burden into the grave. Said evenly, "I've got it, feller," when Max Webster stepped forward to lend a hand.

The bigger man allowed, "I like to do things myself, too."

Edge began to shovel the dirt back into the hole.

"Where did I get to?"

"Old Man Galton bringing just a few grains of gold to Lakeview, feller. Maybe because he was hoarding most of it here on the claim?"

"That's what some folks used to say," Webster muttered and almost pushed his hat off when he scratched the side of his head. Then he shook his head. "But there ain't no one ever did really believe that, sir. Stands to reason. Man that spends most of his life out here in the wilds breakin' his back digging rock outta the ground ain't gonna—"

"So you and the others came around the lake happy with just the twenty bucks advance?" Edge said.

Webster nodded his head vigorously and grinned, like he was happy somebody else had unexpectedly supplied the answer to a question that had been bothering him for a long time. "Yeah, yeah! That's right, sir." But then the happiness went out of his face to leave him looking perplexed. "Then again, the way them Galtons are goin' so hard at it, it figures they believe there's an inheritance out here." Again his features altered their set and he expressed grim determination. "And if there is, I ain't gonna be satisfied with no hundred bucks, I can tell you. I ain't smart, but I ain't that dumb either. I could've got my head blowed off by that shotgun of Mrs. Galton's and I'm gonna want payin' for puttin' my life on the line. Payin' good money, sir. Enough so I can buy a house on the lakefront. And Polly can get herself a husband and don't have to— well, set her cap at men like she did with you."

Edge directed a surreptitious glance at Max Webster and decided the giant of a man was saying exactly what he meant, with no devious hidden intent veiled by the words he spoke and expression he showed.

"The letters Barny Galton wrote his sons mentioned a hoard of gold out here, Max?" Edge asked. And was hit by the thought that perhaps Webster was trying to be devious after all. Was taking the trouble to do all this talking in order to interest him in the doubtful inheritance the father had left his sons. In the event that Lee Galton objected to paying more than a hundred dollars a man to his hired help.

"No, sir. Barny just wrote Lee and Ralph that he figured he was nearin' the end of his time. He wrote he forgave them for not takin' care of him the way sons should. And he said they should come visit him here at the claim. And when they got here, he'd see they had all they needed to last them for the rest of their lives."

Edge completed the dog's grave with several flat-of-the-blade thuds of the shovel at the dirt. Then tossed the shovel away and did not even consider marking the mound with a cross of rocks.

"Guess a letter like that would get me a little stirred up, feller," the half-breed told the bigger man. "If I didn't know the local gossip about the man that wrote it being a little crazy."

"Yeah," Webster agreed dully. Then brightened. "But we ain't got nothin' to lose. We didn't come traveling all the way out here from back

East. We can just stick around and see what turns up in the cabin."

"Uh?"

"That's right, I didn't tell you, did I. Well, after the Galtons done all their talkin' together—when they agreed to go shares in what's found—they got into tryin' to figure out where best to start lookin'. And they reckoned in the cabin. On account of that was where their pa spent his last days. And a man with a fortune hid someplace would want to have it close by him out in a lonely piece of country like this is. So he could protect it against thieves."

He shrugged and looked quizzically at the half-breed, who offered no response. "And anyway, it sure is easier diggin' in the dirt floor of the cabin than out in them mine tunnels." Another shrug. "And that's a fact."

There was a pause then, Max Webster having said as much as he was able without actually asking Edge for help if it was needed. While the half-breed had nothing to say as he cast his mind back to the time spent with the dying old man, trying to recall some word or phrase that might have been a clue to where a hoard of gold dust was hidden on the claim. But he abandoned this search of his memory after just a few moments. For he had no right to such a hoard if it existed, nor any reason to help any of those trying to locate it.

The thick walls of the log cabin continued to trap inside any noise made by the eager searchers. The growing timber did not mask the thud of hooves on sodden ground, which signaled the approach up the trail from the lakeside of a small group of riders.

Webster heard the same hoofbeats and grimaced as he swung around from facing Edge and groaned: "Shit. More trouble and I left my rifle over by—"

An oilskin-garbed form appeared at a corner of the cabin. It was Polly Webster, who shouted in high excitement: "Max! Get over here! They've found somethin'!"

The big man started to run toward his sister as Janet Galton, out of the cabin but out of sight of Edge and Max Webster, shrieked:

"Ralph, there's more company comin', damnit!"

"Guess that'll be the Lakeview sheriff and a posse," Edge said, but Webster was already out of earshot. So the half-breed shrugged and turned to retrieve his Winchester and then began to unhitch the reins of the mare from the clump of brush.

The riders brought their mounts to a halt where the track from the lake entered the clearing on the far side. And Sheriff Herman shouted:

"I'm lookin' for the man named Edge! He still around here, Mrs. Galton?"

The half-breed swung up astride the mare and looked across the clearing behind the cabin. Saw the duster-coated Herman and ten or maybe a dozen other men—three of them draped over and tied to their saddles.

"I'm still here, feller!"

The posse all snapped their heads around to peer, a little fearfully, toward Edge. Tensed to draw guns if the Winchester should be brought down from his shoulder. The half-breed called:

"My horse going to be all right?"

"Frig your horse!" the Lakeview lawman snarled and heeled his mount out of the group —trailing on lead lines the three with corpses for riders. "I told you not to take the law into your own—"

"Eddie Herman, it was them or Edge and me!" Polly Webster cut in, torn between the need she felt to defend the half-breed and an eagerness to follow her brother back into the cabin.

Inside of which, voices were raised in high excitement. Once more each competing with the others to be heard, with the result that little real sense could be made of the occasional snatch that sounded in isolation.

". . . I got it . . ."

"Hot damn, this is . . ."

"Lid's clear . . ."

". . . locked . . ."

"No!"

"Shit, we got it!"

"Bring the . . ."

". . . Janet . . ."

"Polly, come see . . ."

Then, as the woman made to turn to respond to her brother's eager call and the grim-faced Herman with the posse following closed with the impassive Edge, the cabin exploded.

With an ear-splitting crack and an earth-shuddering blast, the roof was tossed high and the walls collapsed inwards. A great tongue of yellow flame licked up at the violently detached

roof—seemed to grip it and jerk it back down, but
in a thousand pieces. This debris hidden in a
twisting ball of black smoke that followed the
flame into the night sky. Went much higher and
did not return, as the flame had returned to become many smaller tongues of fire. Yellow, red,
blue, and green now. Roaring as the dry inner
sections of the collapsed cabin were burned.
Hissing as the rain-sodden outsides were steam
dried before being consumed.

Polly Webster had been knocked to the ground
by the blast. And those men who were not blown
from their saddles had been thrown from them as
the horses reared in panic at the sound, sight,
and smell of the explosion.

And for stretched seconds, as pieces of debris
showered down over a wide area of the clearing,
they all remained pressed to the storm-dampened
ground. Hands instinctively clasped over their
heads. Some curled up into the smallest possible
size. In as much danger from the pumping hooves
of widly bolting horses as from blasted chunks of
timber.

Then the final piece of shattered cabin roof
thudded to the ground. All but two of the horses,
which had bolted blindly down the trail, were
confined by the trap of the trees and the cliff rim
to scraping at the ground, tossing their heads,
and snorting as outlets for their fear. And the fire
was less forceful in the speed and sounds with
which it continued with the destruction of the
cabin.

"Dear God, Max!" Polly Webster shrieked as
she staggered upright and swung around—made

to run toward the blaze but was beaten back by the heat.

"Everyone okay?" Herman yelled as he rolled over and sat up, rubbing at a leg where a piece of falling log had hit him. He made an anxious survey of his posse, all of whom moved to sit or stand up. Calling the names of friends and responding with their own.

"Hell, look at my buggy!" a man yelled angrily and pointed a shaking arm at the overturned rig with a wheel gone and the shafts snapped.

"Frig your buggy, Ephraim Browning!" another man snarled. "Billy Kitteridge and Sam Nelson was in that shack! And the Hall kids! And poor old Max Webster!"

"Wantin' to be rich old Max Webster!" another member of the posse growled as all of them rose to their feet.

Polly Webster dropped despairingly to her knees, arms loose at her sides and head bowed.

Edge finished talking softly to the chestnut mare to calm her, while he continued to rub at his wrist, bruised when the blast threw him against a tree.

"That crazy old bastard must've rigged some kinda box to blow when it was opened up," a Lakeview man called.

"Shit, Barny Galton must've bought near fifty sticks of that dynamite off me this past year!" another shouted. "One or two at a time. Figured he was usin' them in his mine tunnels."

"Planned it all that time back."

"Must've had a real hate for them sons of his."

"Didn't like Lakeview folks much, but he

couldn't've known some of them would be in the shack when it—"

"He was crazy, wasn't he? Hated everyone and everythin' except for that dog of his. Craziest man I ever did come across."

"I reckon everyone's crazy about something," the town's lawman said dully as his first contribution to the discussion.

This after he had balefully watched Edge check that the mare was not injured. Then mount the horse and take out the makings to roll a cigarette.

When the cigarette was lit, the half-breed blew out the match and flicked it toward the fresh grave. Told Herman: "Dog was heading back here when he was running scared. Place he felt safest at, I figure."

"One of the gunslingers kill him?"

"Edge killed him," Polly Webster answered suddenly as she rose to her feet, but continued to face the heap of charred debris. "Because the animal started to eat one of the corpses."

Herman grimaced and swallowed hard. Then accused with a sneer, "Harder than killing a man, was it?"

"What needs to be done, needs to be done, sheriff," the half-breed replied evenly. "I asked you already about my horse?"

The lawman spat before he said: "John Payne says your horse'll be fit to ride in a couple of days, mister. But you can walk him out of Lakeview any time you're ready. No charge. All the money you left is in your saddlebags back at Frank Benson's livery stable. John Payne don't want no part of blood money."

"Then that's some more I have to have somebody put in the town poor box, feller," Edge answered tautly. "Always pay my way. Some way."

"Ain't nothin' wrong with bounty money," Polly Webster growled. "Not when it's earned killin' the kind of men you found back on the trail, Eddie Herman. That were fixin' to shoot me down like a—"

"You want to go tell Mary Benson that, Polly?" the sheriff cut in sourly. "This bounty hunter hadn't come to Lakeview, those three wouldn't have followed and Frank would still be alive."

"It happens!" the woman replied as she at last turned away from the burning remains of the cabin, the smoke from which was beginning to carry the sickly sweet aroma of over cooked human meat. "If Barny Galton hadn't sent them letters to his sons and got more than just Ralph and Lee stirred up about a pile of gold . . ." Her features formed into a familiar expression of sourness as she glanced once more at the scene of blackened destruction. Then looked around just as briefly at the grim-faced posse, the scowling Herman, and the impassive Edge. To finish on a low note: "Greed and hatred is what's led to all the killin' and grief that's happened. Been the same since the world began, my opinion."

Now she searched the clearing with her eyes for her horse, saw the gelding over near the rock outcrop, and went to get him.

The Lakeview lawman sighed with weary resignation and massaged both his bristled cheeks as he growled: "Yeah, all right, Polly. Have it your way!"

"Seems to me, Eddie," a member of the posse muttered, "the only one that had it his way was Barny Galton."

"And look what happened to him," Herman recalled with a brief grimace as he began to gather together the horses with dead bodies draped over their saddles. "He lost out on seeing the way things finished."

Edge took a final draw against his cigarette and dropped it to the wet ground, where it sizzled out. Resisted an urge to glance over to where he had dug two graves. Heeled the mare into movement and tried not to be conscious that there was no German shepherd following him.

"And what a finish," a man rasped.

"Yeah," the half-breed murmured for just his own ears, which heard better than his eyes were seeing as he glanced at the charred debris that covered eight fire-blackened corpses before he turned to gaze directly ahead. A dead heat.

EDGE

BY
George G. Gilman

More bestselling
western adventure from Pinnacle,
America's #1 series publisher.
Over 8 million copies of EDGE in print!